' You will join m
secretary,' he dra
know that you'll
role quite perfectly... as my *mistress*.'

'But Riccardo—'

'No, say nothing more—for I will not countenance your objections. It is the perfect solution,' he mused. 'You can provide me with sweet delight to distract me from all the stultifying details of the forthcoming wedding.'

'But why, Riccardo?' she breathed. 'I mean, why *me*?'

Almost impartially he studied her, and it was then that Angie realised how cold a colour black could be—for his eyes looked positively icy as they flicked over her distressed face.

'Because you have unlocked a certain inexplicable *hunger* in me, *cara mia*—and I see no reason not to feed that hunger until we are both satisfied. You have already decided to leave my employment, so let us make sure that when you do it is with no lasting regrets on either side.'

Sharon Kendrick started story-telling at the age of eleven, and has never really stopped. She likes to write fast-paced, feel-good romances, with heroes who are so sexy they'll make your toes curl! Born in west London, she now lives in the beautiful city of Winchester—where she can see the cathedral from her window (but only if she stands on tiptoe). She has two children, Celia and Patrick, and her passions include music, books, cooking and eating—and drifting off into wonderful daydreams while she works out new plots!

Recent titles by the same author:

CONSTANTINE'S DEFIANT MISTRESS
BOUGHT FOR THE SICILIAN BILLIONAIRE'S BED
SICILIAN HUSBAND, UNEXPECTED BABY
THE GREEK TYCOON'S CONVENIENT WIFE

THE ITALIAN BILLIONAIRE'S SECRETARY MISTRESS

BY
SHARON KENDRICK

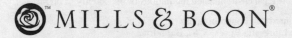

All the characters in this book have no existence outside the imagination of the author, and have no relation whatsoever to anyone bearing the same name or names. They are not even distantly inspired by any individual known or unknown to the author, and all the incidents are pure invention.

First published in Great Britain 2009
Harlequin Mills & Boon Limited,
Eton House, 18-24 Paradise Road, Richmond, Surrey TW9 1SR

© Sharon Kendrick 2009

ISBN: 978 0 263 87435 8

Set in Times Roman 10½ on 12¾ pt
01-1009-43794

Harlequin Mills & Boon policy is to use papers that are natural, renewable and recyclable products and made from wood grown in sustainable forests. The logging and manufacturing process conform to the legal environmental regulations of the country of origin.

Printed and bound in Spain
by Litografia Rosés, S.A., Barcelona

THE ITALIAN BILLIONAIRE'S SECRETARY MISTRESS

CHAPTER ONE

MAYBE because it was nearly Christmas and the sharp, cold weather had jolted her senses. Or maybe because she'd just had enough. But something had to change. It *had* to.

Angie's fingers trembled and she looked at them curiously, as if they belonged to someone else. But no, those neat, unvarnished nails belonged to her—a foolish woman with an empty heart which ached for a man who was beyond her reach. Who barely even noticed she was a member of the opposite sex—and treated her as he might treat one of his many powerful cars. And while Riccardo treated his cars with care—she wasn't an inanimate, functional *object*, was she? She was a living, breathing woman with desires of her own which were never going to be met. She had to leave him—she *had* to. Because if she wasn't careful she was going to waste her whole life loving a man who could never love her back. And sooner or later even her dreams would be smashed when he picked a suitable bride from all the actresses and models he'd dated over his action-packed life.

Riccardo Castellari, her boss—and the man who pretty much haunted her every waking thought. Well, not for much longer. Come the New Year and she was going to start looking for a new job—far away from the dizzy distraction of the black-eyed Italian who could make a woman swoon at a hundred paces with just a flick of that lazy smile. Except that he hadn't been smiling much lately. His mood had been dark—his short temper more frayed than usual and, unusually, Angie wasn't sure why.

'Cheer up, Angie—it's nearly Christmas!'

As the words of the junior secretary cut into her thoughts Angie summoned up a smile. 'It certainly is,' she agreed softly as she looked around the staffroom.

Nearly Christmas and the normally tasteful offices of Castellari International were decked out with seasonal holly and the occasional hopeful sprig of mistletoe. When he'd first set up the London headquarters of his highly lucrative global business, Riccardo had banned tinsel on the grounds of bad taste. But gradually he'd given in to popular demand as garish strand after garish strand was introduced with every year which passed. This year the staffroom seemed to resemble Santa's Grotto, thought Angie wryly—and some of the offices weren't much better.

Glittering silver, gold, scarlet and greens were looped around every available picture and door jamb and fairy lights festooned the fax machines. The coffee shop down the road was playing corny Christmas songs all day and yesterday the Salvation Army band had stood in the square and played carols so soaringly beautiful that Angie had had to swallow back tears as she'd fished around in her purse for a crumpled five-pound note.

Yes, it was nearly Christmas, and wasn't that part of the whole problem—and the reason why she was feeling so emotionally wobbly? Because Christmas did something to the world at large and to individuals in particular. It crystallised all your hopes and fears. It made you yearn and wish and dream. And no matter how hard you tried—it made you realise all the things you were missing in life.

'Are you looking forward to tonight's office party?' asked the junior, a sweet young secretary named Alicia who'd only joined a few months ago.

Angie pulled a face of mock-horror. 'Are you kidding?'

Alicia looked at her eagerly. 'What's it like? Everyone says it's absolutely fantastic—one of London's classiest restaurants and with no expense spared! And is it true that Mr Castellari stays for the whole time?'

Angie had had enough experience of juniors being slightly overawed by her boss. Hadn't she once been like Angie herself? Sneaking glances at his dark, beautiful face from afar and wondering how a man ever got to be that gorgeous. The only difference was that she had been plucked out of the typing pool by Riccardo himself

and elevated to the dizzy status of his secretary overnight. She wasn't quite sure *why* he'd chosen her—she
had just been overjoyed that he had. And now? Well,
now she wasn't so sure. Sometimes she thought her life
would be less complicated if she had stayed put in the
typing pool. That way she would have moved on by
now, gone to pastures new—and far away from the in-
toxicating presence of the sexy Italian.

She smiled at Alicia. 'He certainly does. He's there
right until the end.' Or the *bitter* end, as Riccardo rather
bitingly put it. Truth to tell, he wasn't crazy on
Christmas—but once a year he put himself out and ful-
filled all the expectations of the Castellari workforce.
He lavished money on a party which still had people
talking in February and he gave everyone a generous
bonus. Even her. Though hadn't she sometimes longed
for him to give her something a little more…*personal*?

Recognising that there was no sense in longing for
the impossible, Angie stood up and flicked a tiny piece
of fluff from the front of her jersey skirt. 'In fact, I'd
better go and finalise a few arrangements—I'm expecting Riccardo back any time now.'

'*Are* you?' questioned Alicia enviously.

'Yes. He's on his way from the airport.' Angie knew
his schedule down to the last second. The dark limousine would be speeding its way towards central London
and Riccardo would be stretching his long legs out in
the back. He would have loosened his tie and he might
be flicking through some paperwork. Or talking on the

phone in one of the three languages he spoke. He might even be exchanging a few desultory comments with his Italian-speaking driver, Marco—who doubled as a bodyguard when the need arose.

'In fact…' Angie glanced at her watch '…if the roads are clear, then he might be—' Her beeper began emitting a high-pitched little squeal and she could do absolutely nothing about the rapid acceleration of her heart. 'Excuse me,' she said, with a brisk little smile which hid her instinctive excitement, 'but he's in the building.'

On her low-heeled, perfectly polished navy shoes, she sped along to her office which adjoined Riccardo's—a breath of pleasure escaping her lips as she walked into the light and spacious room. Because it didn't matter how many times she saw it, she could never get over the fact that she worked in a place as beautiful as this. It was, Angie reflected, like a picture postcard come to life.

The Castellari headquarters looked out over the vast and impressive space of Trafalgar Square and the world-famous landmark always looked beautiful with its pluming fountain and tall statue, but never more so than at Christmas time. The iconic fir tree sent over each year by the King of Norway twinkled brightly and every single window as far as the eye could see was alive with brightly coloured Christmas lights. Angie stared out of the window. It looked…magical.

But then she heard the sound of a familiar footfall ringing along the corridor. A footfall she would have recognised even if it were treading in thick snow and she quickly moved into his office to greet him, wiping all traces of wistfulness from her face and replacing it with the calm and efficient expression which Riccardo had learned to expect from his right-hand woman. But nothing could stop the sudden acceleration of her heart as the door opened and she looked into his dark, heart-breakingly handsome face.

'Ah, Angie. You are here. Good.' His deep, accented voice washed over her skin like raw silk as he dropped his briefcase and coat onto one of the squashy leather sofas. His black hair was tousled as if he had been running his fingers through it and he had loosened his tie as she'd known he would. A brief smile was slanted in her direction and then he picked up a sheaf of papers and began flicking through them. 'Get me the paperwork on the Posara takeover bid, would you?'

'Certainly, Riccardo,' she replied smoothly as she automatically scooped up the beautiful cashmere coat and hung it up.

Did her features betray her probably unreasonable hurt—that the man she had not seen for a fortnight should barely deign to greet her? Not a *hello* or a *how are you*? If she had been substituted by one of the other secretaries, would he even have *noticed*? But good secretaries didn't obsess about the fact that they might as well have been invisible for all the notice that was taken of them. And she prided herself on being a good secretary.

'Good trip?' she asked politely as she deposited the file he wanted onto the centre of his desk.

He shrugged. 'New York is New York. You know. Busy, buzzy, beautiful.'

Angie didn't know, as it happened—because she'd never been there. 'I suppose it must be,' she observed politely, biting down the question she longed to ask. About whether or not he'd seen Paula Prentice—the woman all the papers had been linking him to a year ago. Paula with her blonde and tanned beauty, her amazingly white teeth and a body which had been voted Most Lusted After by a leading men's magazine.

When Riccardo had been dating the Californian lovely, he had spent many weekends in the Big Apple—and Angie would anxiously study his face on his return, wondering if he was going to announce that he was planning to make the stunning Paula his bride. But he hadn't. To Angie's enormous relief, they'd split—again, according to the papers, since Riccardo certainly didn't discuss his private life with his secretary.

'And how about the de Camilla account?' she questioned, because that, after all, was the deal he'd gone out there to oversee.

'*Frustrante!* Frustrating,' he translated, tugging his silk tie off completely as he glanced up at her.

'I could just about work that out for myself, Riccardo.'

'Oh?' Jet dark brows were elevated. Did his sensible, reliable mouse of a secretary have frustrations in her own life? he wondered. He doubted it. The only frustrations he could imagine *her* having were being unable to find a new knitting pattern. Or her television breaking down, perhaps. He glittered her an ebony glance. 'You have been taking the crash course in Italian, perhaps?'

'Hardly! My Italian may be poor but I have a comprehensive knowledge of exclamations and profanities which I've managed to acquire after working for you for so long!' she said crisply. 'Now, would you like some coffee?'

Riccardo gave the ghost of a smile. 'I would *love* some coffee—could you tell?'

Hopelessly, she noted the way his voice dipped when he said *love* like that. 'Of course I could, because—'

'Because?'

'You're entirely predictable.'

'Am I?'

'As the sun which rises in the morning sky. And in a minute you'll start moaning about the fact that tonight's the office party—'

'It's *tonight*?' Riccardo raked long olive fingers through already tousled black hair. *'Madonna mia!'*

'You see?' she murmured as she walked over to the machine which had been exported here at great expense from his native Italy. 'Entirely predictable.'

Ignoring the file in front of him, Riccardo sat back and watched her for a moment, thinking that she was the only woman whom he would allow occasionally to tease him. She was certainly a lot less timid than when he had first employed her—though her dress sense hadn't improved one little bit. Disparagingly, he flicked a glance over her neat skirt and the pristine blouse which accompanied it and he suppressed a very Italian shudder. How dull she looked! But perhaps he was ill-advised to criticise her appearance under the circum-stances. After all—hadn't her plainness been one of the reasons he'd employed her?

He'd been looking for someone to replace the motherly figure who had guarded his office since his arrival in London but who was leaving to spend time with her grandchildren, no matter how much he'd tried to persuade her otherwise.

It had been a gruelling day of interview after inter-view—when it had seemed that every would-be glamour model in the universe had tried to convince him that she wanted nothing more but to type his letters and answer the phone. He hadn't believed one of them—not when their accompanying actions had belied the sin-cerity of their words.

Riccardo knew what he wanted, and he did not want distractions in the office—women crossing and uncross-ing their legs to show him peeps of stocking tops, or leaning forward to accentuate their cleavage. In fact, he regarded his time at work as a break from the constant attentions of women which had plagued him since his early teens.

The afternoon interviewing session which had fielded a clutch of admirably qualified graduates had proved no more fruitful in his search to find someone prepared to work for him on *his* terms. Not one of them had flinched when he had flicked a cool, challenging gaze and stated that what he wanted was an old-fashioned secretary. Not an assistant—and certainly not an equal. He was not interested in teaching them anything and there would be no fast-track promotion through the business.

His outrageous assertion had not put off a single candidate and yet Riccardo had moodily rejected every one of them—mainly on the illogical grounds that there wasn't one he couldn't have bedded before the evening was out. And he wanted a secretary, not a lover.

But then he had been on his way home and had passed the open door of the typing pool—to see some mouse of a thing bent over the filing cabinet. To a man with the Italian sensibilities of Riccardo, her appearance was appalling—a functional skirt which did her no favours and hair scraped back into an unflatteringly tight bun.

He remembered glancing at his watch, thinking how late it was and admiring her dedication to duty before deciding that she probably didn't have much to rush home to; this mouse was unlikely to have a line of men beating their way to her door. Maybe she was one of those women who lived at the office, he thought wryly.

She must have been alerted to his presence for she had whirled round, fingers flying to her bare lips—her cheeks colouring a rosy-pink when she saw him standing there. It was a long time since a woman had blushed in his presence and for a moment a faint smile had played around Riccardo's lips.

'Can I…can I help you, sir?' she had questioned with

the kind of deference which told him that she knew exactly who he was.

'Maybe you can.' His eyes had narrowed as he took in the dreary surroundings of the communal room and then back to study her surprisingly long fingers. 'Can you type?'

'Yes, sir.'

'Fast?'

'Oh, yes, sir.'

'And what would you say,' he had asked, 'if I asked you to make me a coffee?'

Angie's eyelids had lowered by a deferential fraction. 'I would ask if you took it black or white, sir,' she had replied softly.

Riccardo had smiled. So—she had no unrealistic ambitions to be on the board. Or none of the ridiculous modern attitude which meant that women no longer seemed prepared to wait on men!

She had been installed in his office the very next day— and up until this moment she was the best secretary he'd ever had. Mainly because she knew her place and had no desire to leave it. And perhaps just as importantly because she hadn't fallen in love with him—although naturally she adored him, as women invariably did.

His recollection faded as the tantalising aroma of coffee reached him and Angie put a cup of coffee in front of him. Cappuccino, because it was before noon. Just as later she would produce an inky-black espresso after lunch. She acted like balm to a troubled flare of skin, he thought suddenly. Like a long, warm bath after a transatlantic flight. For a moment, he relaxed. But only for a moment.

His time in New York had been troublesome—with the actress he had dated earlier in the year refusing to accept that it was over. Why did women show such little dignity when a man ended a relationship? he wondered bitterly. And there were problems at home in Tuscany, too…

'Riccardo?' Angie's soft voice drifted into his troubled thoughts.

'What?'

She stood there looking at him—wondering what was causing his darkly handsome face to look so grim. 'You do know that the party's starting a little earlier this year?'

'Don't nag, Angie.'

'It's called a timely reminder.'

He bit back a sigh of irritation. 'What time?'

'We start at seven-thirty.'

'And the restaurant's booked?'

'Everything's ready. I'm going there now just to check a few last-minute details. All you have to do is turn up.'

He nodded. Maybe he could grab a little sleep. 'I'll go back to my apartment and change,' he said. 'And then go straight to the restaurant. There's nothing especially urgent that I need to handle here, is there?'

'Nothing that can't wait until Monday.'

She turned to leave and as he noticed the plain navy skirt which hung so unflatteringly over her bottom

Riccardo suddenly remembered the package he had left lying in the car.

'Oh, Angie?'

'Yes, Riccardo?'

'You don't usually bother dressing up, like the other girls, do you?' he questioned slowly. 'For the office party, I mean.'

Angie halted, composing her face before she turned to face him with just the right amount of friendly interest. It wasn't just that the question was so unexpected—it *was*—it was just extremely hurtful into the bargain, though she was pretty sure he didn't mean it to be. Of *course* she dressed up for the party—but her taste was different from the other girls'. Inevitably. Because so was her age. When you were barely into your twenties you could easily buy up one of the cheap and sequined dresses which abounded in the shops at this time of year. You could splash out very little on an entire outfit—and end up looking like a million dollars.

But when you were twenty-seven, it was a little different. You ran the risk of looking tacky. Or like mutton dressed as lamb. So Angie handled her budget carefully and dressed accordingly. All her clothes were conservative pieces. Investment dressing, they called it. Clothes that would never date—which you could bring out year after year and they would look just as smart. Why, last year she had been wearing a lovely beige knitted dress—with a string of real pearls around her neck.

'Oh, I just throw on any old thing,' she responded, determined that he should not see how hurt she was.

'Well, I have a present for you in the car,' he said softly. 'I'll speak to Marco on the way out and have him deliver it up here for you.'

Angie blinked. A *present*? Normally, he gave her vouchers along with her Christmas bonus. And a case of wine from his family's vineyard in Tuscany—most of which still lay untouched from last year. But he'd never bought her anything *personal* before. Her heart lifted—even though the thought came into her head that perhaps he was trying to sweeten her up. Had he maybe guessed that she was thinking of leaving him and so was trying to induce her to stay? No, Riccardo would never be that subtle.

'Gosh,' she said, and shrugged her shoulders in helpless pleasure—completely unsure how to react. 'What kind of present?'

His eyes ran over her assessingly, and he smiled. 'Something to wear,' he murmured. 'Something for the party.'

CHAPTER TWO

ANGIE gasped as she peeled back the final layer of tissue paper and pulled the dress from the shiny box, her cheeks flaring as scarlet as the fine silk-satin which slipped through her fingers. And suddenly she felt glad she was alone. Glad that nobody was around to see—because surely Riccardo wasn't seriously proposing she wear *this*?

It was the kind of dress which usually featured in the glossy pages of aspirational magazines—and even Angie had heard of the designer whose name was embroidered so beautifully on the label. She swallowed. This gown must have cost a small fortune. For a brief, mad moment the thought sped through her mind that she might be able to sell it on one of the many internet auction sites. But what if Riccardo found out? Would that look awfully rude—his secretary ungratefully flogging a present which had clearly cost him a lot of money?

She held it up to the light. It felt so gossamer-light it shimmered like some kind of rich red syrup, and a feeling she'd never had before crept over her. It was curiosity and it was wistfulness and it was a desire to know whether someone like her could carry it off. Shouldn't she just try it on? Just to see. Slipping into the en-suite bathroom where Riccardo sometimes took a shower if he was going straight out to dinner from the office, Angie locked the door and then stripped off her skirt and blouse.

The first thing which became apparent was that it was the kind of dress where it was impossible to wear a bra—unless you happened to have one of those backless, halter-neck bras, which Angie most certainly didn't. Her underwear was as practical as the rest of her wardrobe. Pants and bras made in fabrics whose main function was to show no visible panty line.

Rather furtively, she removed her bra and then slithered into the dress just as she heard someone entering the office and she froze in absolute horror. Riccardo hadn't told her he was expecting anyone!

'Hello?' she called out nervously.

'Angie?'

Cautiously, Angie opened the door and put her head round to see young Alicia standing there and she let out a sigh of relief. 'Yes, what is it?' she questioned briskly, though it was difficult sounding efficient when this buttery-soft fabric was whispering against her skin like a sensual kiss.

Alicia was blinking. 'What are you doing?'

For a moment it occurred to Angie to tell the junior secretary that it was none of her business what she was doing. But mightn't Alicia tell her the truth? 'Will you give me your honest opinion on what I'm thinking of wearing to the party?' she questioned.

Alicia smiled. 'Of course.'

Angie stepped out into the office and the minute she saw Alicia's shell-shocked face she knew that she'd been right to ask. 'I'll go and take it off.'

'Don't you *dare*,' said Alicia fiercely. 'Come and stand in the light and let me see you properly. Oh, Angie—I can't believe it's really you. You look…you look *gorgeous*.'

No one had ever called her gorgeous before and Angie wouldn't have been human if she hadn't allowed herself to bask in the unexpected—if rather back-handed—compliment. But then she caught sight of herself in the large mirror which reflected back the London skyline and she stared at herself in disbelief. She had never really understood why women were prepared to pay hundreds and hundreds of pounds for a garment which could be reproduced for a modest sum in just about any high street store, but suddenly she did. Because how on earth could a simple piece of fabric be fashioned to make the wearer look so…so…

Angie swallowed. The scarlet satin seemed to mould her skin like cream poured over a peach and the rich material skated over her bottom and clung to her bust. It should have looked tarty and yet it didn't—for the material was rich and the gown seemed to accentuate qualities she hadn't even known she possessed. It sung of sensuality and quality instead of screaming availability.

'Oh, Angie,' breathed Alicia. 'You look like a princess.'

'And I feel like a princess,' Angie responded slowly, before turning away from the mirror with a resolute shake of her head. 'No, I can't possibly wear it.'

Alicia stared at her in disbelief. 'Why ever not?'

'Because…because…' Because, what? Because it made her into an Angie she'd never seen before? One she didn't know and had no idea how to handle? One who felt all kind of squirmy and excited—the way she'd always imagined a woman should feel before a party, but which she couldn't ever remember feeling before? Or because Riccardo had bought this dress? And that was the most incredible thing of all. Riccardo had bought it for her! *Did he imagine me wearing it when he bought it?* she found herself wondering—her heart hammering with an urgent kind of longing. And if that were the case—wouldn't it be wrong *not* to wear it?

'You *have* to wear it,' said Alicia firmly. 'Because you'll never forgive yourself if you don't.'

And so Angie allowed herself to be convinced—telling herself that someone as young and as trendy as Alicia would have told her if she was making a fool of herself. She even allowed herself to be taken along to one of the shops on Oxford Street to buy a pair of towering black stilettos to do the dress justice. And the sweetest little sparkly black clutch bag. Even to take her hair down and to brush it until it gleamed and—although she had always despaired of a colour which most resembled wet sand—she had to agree that it looked rather nice. In fact, she took all the advice that Alicia offered and let her put two coats of mascara onto her eyelashes and to coat her lips in an extravagant-looking gloss.

The trouble was that this high level of preparation took much longer than it normally did and made Angie horribly late. So that instead of being the first to arrive—for once, she was the very last. Usually, she walked into a restaurant and was shown to a corner where she would sit unnoticed, quietly nursing a drink until the others arrived.

But not tonight.

Tonight, as the plate-glass doors of one of the city's most upmarket restaurants slid open, she was aware of something very odd as she put one high-heeled shoe over the threshold. Silence. Complete and utter pindrop silence, before the buzz of conversation resumed. Angie blinked. She was sure she hadn't imagined it.

From nowhere, a waiter appeared at her side and stuck very close to it as she mentioned the name of the Castellari table, his smile very wide indeed as he gestured that she follow him. And Angie sensed that every eye was on her as she made her way through the room. Why were they all looking at her? she wondered in a panic. Surreptitiously, her hand slid round to her bottom, smoothing down her dress—because for one awful moment she had imagined that it was tucked into her tights. But no, all seemed well.

Until she spotted the long, large table containing most of the Castellari workforce and in particular Riccardo, who sat at the head of it—staring at her as she could never remember him staring at her before. And inside, Angie felt a terrible flutter of nerves. What if Riccardo didn't like the dress? Or was embarrassed that he had ever purchased such a personal gift for his secretary?

She slanted him a shy smile which he didn't return. On the contrary. He continued to stare at her with a look of pure astonishment on his face—a look which he didn't bother to hide, even when he curled his finger to beckon her over. She walked across to stand directly in front of him and his eyes flicked over her as if she had suddenly sprouted wings, or horns.

'Is...something wrong?' she questioned hesitantly.

Wrong? Riccardo felt his mouth dry. He wouldn't quite put it like that. It was just that up until this precise moment he'd had no idea that his secretary possessed a pair of the most pert and lush breasts he had ever seen, and the silky fabric was caressing them like a man's tongue. He swallowed. Or that her waist should dip in like that. Or her hips swell out into slim curves, or that she had such a luscious bottom. Or indeed that her legs should be so long...long enough to...

'*Ma che ca...*' he began, and then halted, his face darkening as the waiter murmured something to him in Italian and Riccardo snapped something back so that the man looked taken aback. And all of a sudden Riccardo was pointing peremptorily to the empty space beside him and, not quite believing her luck, Angie slid in next to him. Usually there was a battle royal to sit next to the boss and usually he conferred an imperious nod to the lucky two who would flank him while Angie watched him from afar.

But tonight Riccardo wasn't paying anyone any attention except *her*.

'What the hell are you playing at?' he demanded.

She blinked at him in confusion. His black eyes looked as she'd never seen them before. With distinctly unseasonable anger lurking in their ebony depths—and why the hell was he directing it at *her*? 'What do you mean?'

'You look…' For once, words failed him.

'You don't like the dress, is that it?'

He shook his head. 'No, that is not it,' he bit out, trying and failing to avert his eyes from her creamy décolletage.

'What, then?'

He pulled the napkin over his lap, glad to be able to conceal the lower half of his body. How could he possibly tell her that she didn't look like Angie any more? That he felt relaxed and comfortable with the plain and frumpy Angie—not this sizzling sex-pot of a creature who was attracting the lecherous gaze of every hot-blooded male in the place. And that he was aroused, which was as inconvenient as it was unexpected.

He shook his head. 'I wasn't expecting…'

She had never known Riccardo Castellari tongue-tied before. Never. 'Wasn't expecting *what*?' she challenged, but deep down she knew exactly what he meant, even though the realisation hurt her more than he would ever know. He hadn't been expecting her to look good in it, that was it. Angie was not in the least bit vain—but neither was she stupid. And she'd seen enough of people's reactions tonight—as well as her own reflection in the mirror—to realise that for once her appearance was transformed. And now he was in danger of spoiling her once-in-a-lifetime Cinderella experience with that dark and faintly dangerous expression on his face.

'If you're implying that the outfit is unsuitable for an occasion like this, then remember that *you're* the one who told me to wear it and *you're* the one who bought it for me,' she said tartly.

At this his face darkened even more, and he seemed about to say something else—presumably another insult—but then he nodded, forcing out a lazy smile. 'Forgive me for my lack of manners, Angie. You…you fill the dress very well,' he added slowly, impatiently waving away the bread basket which was doing the rounds.

It was a curious way to put it—and it was a very continental way to put it. It thrilled her to have Riccardo say something like that to her and the last thing in the world she needed was to increase the thrill factor where her boss was concerned. Accepting the glass of champagne which the waiter was offering her, she took a big sip. 'Do I?'

God, yes. Riccardo felt like a man who had just been given a spoonful of bitter medicine—only to discover that it was as sweet as nectar. He had given Angie the dress more as an idle and convenient gesture than anything else—and now she had completely surprised him.

And it was a long time since a woman had surprised him.

Forcing himself to remember that this was the woman who spent more time with him than anyone else, who made his coffee and sorted out the dry-cleaning of his shirts, Riccardo picked up his own glass of champagne rather thoughtfully. Remember too that this is the staff party, he told himself—and that after tonight you don't have to see her until the new year when she'll be back to looking like Angie and you can forget all about the sex-bomb image.

'So what are you doing for Christmas?' he questioned conversationally, willing his erection to subside as he forced himself to spear a large prawn and eat it.

'Oh, you know.' Angie drank some more champagne. It was *delicious*. 'Family stuff.'

Riccardo put his fork down. He certainly did. Sometimes he thought he could write a textbook about families—especially dysfunctional Italian ones. But Angie's would be very different... A wry smile quirked the corners of his lips. 'You'll see your parents, of course? What is it—let me guess—a cosy and very English Christmas around the tree?'

Angie's face didn't change, but she brought the glass up to her lips more as a distraction technique than because she particularly wanted to drink any more of the wine, because it was making her feel a little bit giddy. She forced a smile. 'Well, not really, no. As I'm sure you know—my father is dead and my mother is worried sick because my sister's getting a divorce.'

Riccardo's eyes narrowed as he registered the subtle

dig. *Had* he known that? Had she perhaps told him and it had slipped his mind? He looked at the honeyed spill of her hair and wondered why she didn't wear it down more often. '*Sì, sì*—of course.' He shrugged—for he had wanted a polite, monosyllabic response from her, not to continue with a topic such as this one. But it was nearly Christmas and she deserved his civility. 'And is that a…difficult situation?'

Angie knew her boss well enough to know when he was distracted, when he was asking a question because he felt it was expected of him rather than because he was particularly interested in the answer. And although it was usually in her nature to instinctively accede to Riccardo's wishes, to cushion his life and make it as carefree as possible—tonight she wasn't in a particularly cushioning or secretarial mood. Let him ask something about *her* for a change—for hadn't she devoted enough of her life asking about *him*?

She thought about the actuality of the festival which was looming up. About the frantic phone calls she and her mother would receive from her sister. And their frustration at their powerlessness to do anything much to help because she was so far away. And she thought of Riccardo, who would be flying off to Tuscany—to his family's amazing castle. Unlike her, *his* new year would be filled with lots of exciting things. New challenges. A new woman probably.

'Actually, yes, it is difficult,' she admitted. 'Especially

at Christmas time. Because, if you remember—my sister lives in Australia and we can't be there for her.'

Riccardo leaned back to allow the half-eaten plate of prawns to be replaced with some sort of fish, and viewed it unenthusiastically. 'Yes,' he said. 'I can imagine it can't be easy.'

Angie doubted it. Riccardo had many, many characteristics which made him irresistible to women, but an ability to put himself in someone else's shoes and to empathise wasn't at the top of the list.

Angie leaned closer and peered into his face. 'Can you really?' she questioned pointedly.

Riccardo was so preoccupied with the tantalising glimpse of her cleavage when she leaned forward that he failed to register a word of what she was saying. Or what he had said to her. But she had clearly just asked him a question and so he tried the fail-safe approach which always worked and which women seemed to love.

'Why don't you tell me about it?' he murmured.

Angie's mouth opened into an astonished little 'oh' shape that Riccardo should have given her carte blanche to confide in him. He really *was* being attentive tonight, she thought. Understanding, even. Nobody else was even getting a look-in. And the awful thing was that, try as she might to quell it, she began to get a flicker of hope that he really *might* be thinking of her as a woman at last.

'Well, my sister keeps ringing up in hysterics because it's a really acrimonious divorce,' she said.

Riccardo shrugged. 'Ah, but surely that is the nature

of divorce.' He studied her, aware of the trace of some light perfume which was drifting towards his nostrils. Maybe she always wore perfume…but if that was the case, then why had he never noticed it before? Noticing that one of the waiters seemed to be as fascinated by her as he was, Riccardo glowered at him until he went away again. 'Did they marry for love—your sister and her husband?' he questioned, sitting back in his chair.

'Oh, yes,' said Angie defensively, though the question caught her off guard and she found herself grateful for the candlelight which shielded the sudden rush of colour to her cheeks provoked by Riccardo speaking about *love*.

He shrugged. 'Well, there you have your reason for their break-up in a nutshell.'

She raised her eyebrows. 'I don't know what you mean.'

'Don't you? It's quite simple. Never marry for love. Much too unreliable.'

Someone was enthusiastically poking her in the ribs and Angie turned to half-heartedly pull at a cracker, glad for the momentary disruption which gave her time to gather her thoughts. To formulate some kind of answer. To be sure he wouldn't see her stupid and naïve disappointment that clearly he thought so little of love.

'You don't really believe that, do you, Riccardo?' she questioned, in a deliberately jocular way.

'*Sì, piccola,*' he said softly. 'Absolutely, I do. For it is unrealistic for a man and a woman to commit to a lifetime together based only the temporary excitement of chemistry and lust. And love is just the polite word we use to describe those things.'

'What do you think they *should* do?' she asked tremblingly. 'Go to a marriage broker?'

He ate a little salad. 'I think that a couple should find as many compatible areas in their lives as possible and work hard to keep the marriage going for the sake of the children. Something which is—alas—becoming increasingly rare in these days of easy divorce.' Putting the glass down, he gave a slow smile. 'And of course, you can maximise your chances of marital success.'

He thought he was making marriage sound like a game of cards now—but Angie continued to stare at him in fascination! 'How?'

'By having a bride who's a generation younger than the groom.'

Angie's mouthful of wine threatened to choke her and she could feel her cheeks growing flushed. 'I *beg* your pardon?'

His black eyes mocked her. 'You heard me perfectly well.'

'I thought my ears must be playing tricks with me.'

'But why are you so shocked?' he questioned carelessly. 'Italian men have done this successfully for centuries. My own parents had such a union and a very happy marriage until my father's death. Because such a match ensures the very best combination between the sexes—an experienced man who can educate a young virgin. He will tutor her in the fine art of pleasure and she will give him many child-bearing years.'

Angie's throat constricted. 'You are…are…'

He leaned closer, enjoying her obvious rage, finding that it was turning him on far more than was wise—but suddenly he didn't care. 'Am what, *piccola*?'

'Outrageous. Outdated. Shall I go on?' she retorted, swallowing to try to dampen down the sudden leap of excitement which his proximity had provoked. But wasn't the real reason for her anger not so much a noble championing of women's rights—but the fact that Riccardo's criteria for finding a bride had effectively ruled her out? That she was neither young, nor a virgin. And how pitiful was that? Surely she wasn't imagining that plain Angie Patterson was in with a chance—because if that were the case then leaving his employment wasn't just a half-hearted desire, but a necessity. 'I can't believe you subscribe to such an outdated point of view, Riccardo,' she finished crossly.

But instead of looking chastened by her criticism, he merely smiled like a cat who had been given an entire vat of cream. 'Ah, but I say what I believe—unfashionable or not. And I have never pretended to be any different, Angie,' he murmured.

And that, she thought, just about summed him up. Riccardo had pleased himself all his life—and the combination of looks, brains and charisma had allowed him to do so. Didn't matter that he expressed views which were deeply unfashionable and would be seen by many as out of date. He didn't care because he didn't have to. Rich, powerful and single—he blazed through life exactly as he wanted to and he wasn't about to start changing now. Why should he?

So forget the fancy dress you're wearing and try to forget your unwanted feelings for him, she told herself fiercely. Just be Angie—and set an example to the juniors by enjoying your staff party.

'Who wants to pull another cracker?' she questioned brightly.

Riccardo sat back in his chair and watched her as she fished a gaudy-looking bracelet from the tissue paper of a spent cracker, and good-naturedly put it onto her wrist. But then, she was pretty much always good-natured, he realised. She was one of those backroom kind of people— the unseen and unnoticed ones who quietly kept the wheels of enterprise turning, without seeking any attention or glory for themselves. He could talk to Angie in a way he couldn't talk to other women. Where would the world be without people like her? His eyes narrowed as a disturbing thought popped into his mind without warning. Because God help him if she ever decided to leave.

Did he treat her properly? Did she get from him all the perks a secretary of her standing would expect to receive? His attention was caught by a pale flurry of snowflakes outside the window. Snow was unusual in London and it would be a cold night. His eyes flicked to the scarlet satin and a pulse began to work at his temple. A *very* cold night. Especially in a dress like that.

And just at that moment, he saw yet another waiter look at her with ill-concealed interest on his face. 'How are you getting home?' he questioned suddenly.

Angie stilled. 'Home?' she echoed stupidly, digging a spoon into her little dish of trifle.

'I presume you have one,' came the dry rejoinder. 'Where do you live?'

The question hurt more than it should have done. She knew everything about him. She knew the size shirt he wore, the hotels he liked to stay in and the wine he liked best to drink. She knew the birthdays of his mother, his brother and his sister and always reminded him in plenty of time for him to buy them presents. That she inevitably ended up choosing those presents was neither here nor there—because that was what good secretaries did, wasn't it?

She knew where he liked to ski in winter and where he occasionally basked in summer. She knew that he never ate pudding but occasionally would eat a square of dark, bitter chocolate with his coffee. She even knew which flowers he liked to send women when he was in pursuit— dark pink roses—and an appropriately generous consolation gift when he inevitably ended it—pearl and diamond cluster ear-studs from an international jeweler, and, oh, what pleasure Angie took in the purchase of *those*.

Yet after five years of her pandering to his every whim and making his life as easy as possible Riccardo Castellari *didn't even know where she lived*!

'Stanhope,' she said, putting her spoon down.

'And where's that?'

'It's on the Piccadilly Line—towards Heathrow.'

'But that's miles out.'

'That's right, Riccardo. It is.'

'And how are you getting there?'

How did he think? 'By broomstick,' she giggled.

He frowned. Angie *giggling*? Was she *drunk*? 'I'm serious, Angie,' he growled.

'Oh, all right, then. By Tube.' She tipped her head to one side, aware of the unaccustomed silky fall of hair over her shoulders. 'Same way I always get home.'

He thought of the late-night underground network, chock-a-block with Christmas revelers, and the kind of reception she might expect to get. And his eyes flicked over her surprisingly slim waist, accentuated by a flimsy silk gown which he must have been *insane* to give her. At the way her breasts seemed to be defying gravity by failing to spill out of the damned dress altogether. No wonder the waiters had been circling her like a pack of wolves for most of the evening, until his icy glance had made it very clear that they were jeopardising their tip by doing so. Was he prepared to sit back and let her go alone into the night? Why, it would be like throwing a lamb before lions!

'Come on—get your coat on,' he ordered abruptly. 'I'm taking you home.'

CHAPTER THREE

FOR a moment Angie stared at Riccardo in disbelief, her lips parting as she stared at him. 'You're…you're taking me home?'

His black eyes gleamed. 'I am.'

'You mean on the Tube?' she questioned blankly, trying to imagine her billionaire boss accompanying her down the escalator.

'No, not on the Tube.' He repressed a shudder. 'In my car.'

'You can't take me home in your car,' she objected. 'You've been drinking.'

'I may have been drinking,' he stated grimly, 'but I can hold my drink—something I suspect you cannot. And believe me, there's little that's more unattractive than a woman who is exhibiting signs of being drunk.'

'That's a very chauvinist remark.'

His eyes gleamed. 'But I am a very chauvinistic man, *piccola*—I thought we had already established that?'

Angie swallowed. There was something very *exciting*

about him when he was speaking to her like that. In that kind of half-challenging, half-threatening way. But *piccola* meant small, didn't it? Her mouth turned down at the corners. That was hardly compliment of the year, was it? 'Are you saying I'm drunk?'

'No, but I'm saying you've had enough alcohol to make you behave in a way which is…uninhibited. I don't think you should travel home alone—it's not safe—and I'm not driving, as it happens. That's what I employ Marco to do. Now take your handbag and let's get going.'

Suddenly, he sounded masterful. The way she'd heard him speak to the occasional model he'd dated and who had dropped in at the office on their way to dinner. Angie could see one of the women from the human resources department staring at them with a very peculiar expression on her face. 'Won't…won't people talk—if we leave together?'

He shot her a cool look. 'Why on earth should they?' he questioned indifferently. 'I'm simply giving my secretary a lift home.'

Well, that certainly put *her* in her place!

Marco had the car waiting with the engine running and Angie slid onto the back seat—completely forgetting that she was wearing a hemline about half as short as usual.

A glimpse of delicious thigh was revealed and Riccardo felt the sudden fizz to his blood. Quickly averting his gaze, he turned instead to stare out of the window as they drove westwards on a journey which seemed to take for ever. Lots and lots of tiny houses—all, it seemed, exactly the same, with cars parked nose to nose by the edges of all the narrow roads. The shops looked unexciting and some of them were boarded up for the night. A small gang of youths stood moodily on a street corner, smoking cigarettes.

Riccardo frowned. Surely he didn't pay her so little that she had to live somewhere like this?

The car came to a smooth halt outside a tall house and he turned to see that she was reclining lazily against the seat. Was she asleep? Her head was leaning back against the soft leather head-rest and her lips were more relaxed than he'd ever seen them. As was the soft fall of hair which tumbled over her shoulders. Not quite the brisk and efficient secretary now, he thought, and gently shook her by the shoulder—suddenly aware of the softness of her flesh. And another tantalising glimpse of thigh as she uncrossed her legs.

Angie started into wakefulness from the half-dream she'd been having, lulled into a sleepy state by the warmth of the car and its smooth passage through the streets. Except when she opened her eyes she found that the dream hadn't ended. For there was Riccardo leaning over her. Riccardo with his hard face and all its shifting planes and shadows. His gleaming black eyes and those hard-soft lips which could shift so easily between contempt and sensuality. For a moment she lost herself in that ebony gaze and a strange ache tugged at the pit of her stomach as she allowed herself the recurring fantasy that Riccardo was about to kiss her.

Except that there had been enough fantasies for one day. The dress. The chauffeur-driven car. But midnight was beckoning and the carriage was about to turn into a pumpkin.

She blinked, struggling to sit up from the seductive comfort of the squashy leather seat—aware of her dry throat as she groped around on the floor of the car for her handbag. 'Thanks for the lift.'

'Don't mention it.'

But he made no move to get out, and with her head clearing by the second, Angie suddenly remembered her manners. He'd come *miles* out of his way to bring her here. And she noticed that he'd eaten barely anything at dinner. Offer him coffee, she thought. He's bound to refuse. Because this felt odd. Disorientating. Riccardo *outside her home*!

'Um, would you like a cup of coffee?'

Riccardo had been just about to tell Marco to let her out when something in her question made him pause and bite back his automatic refusal. What was it, he wondered—a desire to see how someone like Angie lived, in a world away from his own? Suddenly and inexplicably, he was intensely curious—like a tourist in a foreign city who had just found a dark and hidden labyrinth and wanted to discover where it led.

'Why not?' he questioned lazily, and leaned across to open the door for her.

For a moment, Angie stilled. In all their years of working together, they had been close—but never this close. So close that some tantalising trace of sandalwood and warm masculinity stole over her like an irresistible thief. Her hands were trembling as she got out of the car, her heart racing as she inserted her key in the lock, trying desperately to remember what kind of state she'd left the place in that morning. Because, yes, she was a naturally tidy person—but she was only human. What if he wanted to use the loo when she knew there were three pairs of panties drying on a line over the bathtub?

She showed him into her sitting room—trying her best to feel proud of her little home, but nothing could stop her from seeing it through *his* eyes. The tiny sitting room with the tired old furniture which she'd done her best to beautify by adding a few brightly coloured throws. But even though she'd applied several coats of paint to the walls nothing could disguise the ugly, embossed wallpaper underneath. Or the fact that the kitchen looked as if it had been frozen in time and transported there from the middle of the last century. Her only concession to the forthcoming holiday season was an armful of holly which she'd bought down at the market and then stuffed into an enamel jug. At least the dark green foliage and scarlet berries injected some living colour into the room.

'I must, just—er—I'll go and put the kettle on!' she announced. She dashed off to do so and after that she performed a swift underwear sweep of the bathroom.

Stuffing the clean panties into the airing cupboard, she was miserably aware of the tired bathtub and the ancient cistern. Please don't let him want to use the bathroom, she prayed.

She returned to the sitting room with a tray of coffee to find Riccardo standing looking out of the window and as he turned round she could do nothing to prevent the great leap of her heart. He had taken off his jacket and hung it over the edge of the sofa and Angie found herself hoping that he wouldn't snag it there. Never had his Italian elegance been more in evidence than here where it contrasted against the humble setting of her home.

Rather helplessly, she handed him a mug—aware that it was slightly faded and bore the legend of a long-ago national sporting triumph. Just as everything in her life was faded. Or was it just seeing Riccardo standing here—so vibrant and so full of colour and charisma— that made her self-doubt loom into the forefront of her consciousness, like a great dark spectre? She waited for him to make some polite comment about her home, but he didn't. He still had that faint air of distraction he'd had for weeks, she realised—a tension and tightness which added up to more than his usual alpha-male alertness.

'Is everything…okay, Riccardo?' she asked him uncertainly.

He had been miles away and his eyes narrowed as his thoughts cleared and he found himself in her dingy little sitting room holding a large cup of coffee in his hand, which he didn't particularly want.

'What makes you ask that?'

'Just that you seem a bit…oh, I don't know. A bit uptight lately. More so than usual.'

His eyes narrowed suspiciously. Was she prying? Stepping into areas which were nothing to do with her? Yet her face was soft with concern, the way it always was. And couldn't he talk to her in a way that he couldn't talk to other women—because the relationship between boss and secretary was uniquely close without being in any way intimate? With Angie he could unburden himself—could she wash away all his worries with her sweet common sense? Putting the untouched mug down on a faded table, he shrugged.

'Just problems at home,' he bit out.

She knew that no matter how long he had lived in London—or anywhere else in the world for that matter—Italy would always be his home, and Tuscany in particular.

'Something to do with your sister's forthcoming wedding?' she guessed.

His eyes narrowed as he shot her a suspicious look. 'How did you know that?'

She ignored the accusatory tone. She knew how intensely private he was about family matters, but surely he realised that she was privy to many of his telephone conversations—especially when he lost his temper? Or did her general invisibility mean that he overlooked even that simple fact?

'I've heard you…' She hesitated.

Black eyes bored into her. 'Heard me *what*, Angie?'

'Having…' she paused, delicately '…discussions.'

Angrily, he slammed the flat of his hand against the flank of his thigh. 'You mean telling my sister how damned lucky she is to have landed herself an aristocrat for a fiancé? To have found a *Duca* who wishes to make her his wife? So that one day soon she will be a *Duchessa*!'

Angie stared at him in dismay. What a terrible *snob* he could be at times, she thought. She'd met his rebellious and bright-eyed sister a couple of times and really couldn't imagine Floriana settling into life as a member of the Italian aristocracy. Looking into Riccardo's suddenly cold mask of a face, she thought what a formidable brother he would be—forever laying down the law and demanding obedience. And she felt a little tug of sympathy for Floriana. A sympathy strong enough to make her defend his sister in her absence. 'But surely this man's position in society isn't as important as her feelings for him. Does she…*love* him?'

Riccardo's lips curved. 'Oh, please—let's not play into that particular fantasy, Angie—especially when I thought I'd made clear my feelings on the subject of "love" in the restaurant earlier. Aldo adores her. He is a wealthy man with many centuries of breeding behind him—and he has provided Floriana with a stability in her life which was sorely lacking. It is an honour that he has selected my sister as his bride! He will provide for her an excellent home and lifestyle—while she will give him the heir he undoubtedly needs to continue the bloodline,' he finished.

'*Bloodline?*' she echoed incredulously.

'You have a problem with that, do you?'

'It seems a curiously *cold*-blooded way to look at a marriage.'

'It is not cold-blooded—it is simply *practical*,' he snapped. 'But I suppose you know better, do you, Angie— with your vast experience of matters matrimonial?'

The cruel remark hurt, as no doubt it was meant to—but it fired up Angie's indignation, too. Why, he sounded as if he was marrying off his poor sister to the highest bidder!

'Isn't there something vital you've forgotten to mention?' she demanded. 'You're dismissive of love— but what about passion? Is there any of that?'

Passion.

The word dropped into his consciousness like a rock hurled into a still pool and it set off a reaction just like the rippling of waves. A strange word for the mousey Angie to use and yet a word which seemed gloriously appropriate since she was wearing the very colour which denoted passion.

He felt the quickening of his pulse and the sudden pooling of heat at his groin—just as he had done in the restaurant earlier. Temptation mocked him—reminding him that the sweet pleasures of the body seemed nothing but a distant memory these days. With a start, he realised how long it had been since he had lain with a woman and, unthinkably, his gaze flicked over the creamy dé-colletage of the woman who stood in front of him. White skin against scarlet silk.

'Passion?' he echoed as a pulse began a stealthy beat at his temple. 'What do you know about passion?'

'I…I read books,' she answered quickly, aware that she might really have overstepped the mark.

'Only books?' he taunted softly.

And all at once, Angie became aware of a different mood entering the atmosphere—a mood both darkly dangerous and yet intensely exciting. Was it her imag-ination or had Riccardo's lean body tightened, so that suddenly he looked watchful and alert? Like an athlete in peak condition who was mentally preparing himself for the race ahead. His dark eyes were raking over her just as they had done when he'd first seen her in the dress he'd bought her—but now the look seemed underpinned with something else. Something which even she recog-nised was doing a very passable imitation of desire.

Her senses quickened and she felt the rise of colour to her cheeks. Suddenly, she felt out of her depth—the reality of her situation bizarre. It was all *wrong* him being here—with Marco waiting outside in the limou-sine. She felt like someone who was staring into dark and swirling waters—who had only just understood the dangers of jumping in.

'Look, it's getting late and I mustn't keep you any more. Thanks…thanks very much for the lift, Riccardo,' she said uncertainly. 'And for the dress, of course. I love it.' But even as she said it Angie knew that she would probably never wear that dress again. Where did she ever go which would warrant it—without standing out from the crowd, which she hated? And it wasn't *her*. Why would a woman like her wear a dress which probably cost as much as her entire monthly mortgage repayment?

'My pleasure,' he said, trying to ignore the stabbing ache at his groin which was hardening by the second. But the suddenly wistful expression on her face made him feel even more uncomfortable. Should he tell her to stop making such a big deal out of the dress? Tell her that…

'Angie,' he said softly as he noticed the faint tremble of her lips.

She had never heard that note in his voice before. 'What?' she whispered as she lifted her face to look at him—at the hard, beautiful features she knew and loved so well.

The movement of her head made him acutely aware of her perfume and Riccardo found he could not prevent himself from breathing it in, just as he could not tear his eyes away from the sight of her loose hair, which swayed like an armful of ripe corn. Her eyes were darker tonight—not like Angie's eyes at all—and her lips gleamed at him with a provocation he had never noticed in them before. He scented danger on so many levels—but he couldn't seem to move away from it. Or maybe he was just rendered powerless by her sleek, scarlet-clad body, which was sending out a siren call to him which was as old as time itself.

And suddenly Riccardo felt himself overcome with a lust too strong to resist and he gave into the over-whelming desire to pull her into his arms—even while he was telling himself that this was wrong. Telling himself that this mustn't happen. That she would stop it. Sensible Angie wouldn't let this happen.

But Angie seemed to have taken the night off from being sensible. Because now her eyes were fixed on his face with a look of intensity which seemed to echo the way he was feeling inside—and she was biting her lip as if trying to suppress an urgent kind of hunger. A hunger he recognised instantly because it echoed his own. And suddenly he was lowering his head and was kissing her—and she was kissing him back as if her life depended on it.

CHAPTER FOUR

RICCARDO'S mouth drove down on Angie's and she shuddered beneath the sweet pressure of his lips—because the potent power of that kiss exceeded every fantasy she'd ever had about the man. And she'd had more than her fair share of *those*.

Riccardo was kissing her! *Her!* A million stars exploded in her head and the blood fizzed hotly around her veins. Was she *dreaming*?

But no. Dreams—no matter how realistic—did not make your heart pound so fiercely that you felt as if its muffled thunder might deafen you. Nor your knees buckle like someone who'd just got out of bed after a long dose of debilitating flu. Dreams did not conjure up with such vivid accuracy the sensation of your gorgeous Italian boss running his hands up and down your body as if he had every right to do so.

'Oh,' she moaned, unable to believe that this was really happening—that she was in Riccardo Castellari's arms and being kissed so long and so thoroughly that she thought she might faint from the sheer pleasure of it. It should have felt all wrong and yet she couldn't ever remember anything feeling so right. Her fingers fluttered up to clutch at his shoulders as his hands moved to splay themselves over her buttocks and she pressed herself luxuriantly against his powerful frame, unable to bite back her pleasure at the intimate caress. *'Oh!'*

'You like that?' he ground out as he tore his mouth away from hers.

'Oh, yes. *Yes!*'

Almost helplessly, Riccardo closed his eyes as she pressed her body even closer. He could feel the soft weight of her breasts as they pushed against him, their blatant invitation taking him by surprise. He had not planned to kiss her and he could not possibly have guessed the strength of his own response to that kiss. By rights, he should now be beating a hasty retreat from here—blaming the wine and the cloying sentimentality of Christmas time for something which should never have happened. But he didn't feel a bit like that. The very opposite, in fact—because his hunger was building with swift sweetness and heading towards the inexorable path of fulfilment.

'Riccardo,' she breathed helplessly, her breath warm against his ear.

It was the way that she whispered his name that sealed his fate. Before that he still might have been able to terminate this craziness here and now—had not that little moan laid a fresh assault on his senses.

'What?' he questioned huskily. 'What is it?'

The bold words seemed to tumble out of their own accord—but how could they not, when she seemed to have spent a whole lifetime repressing them? 'I…I want you.'

'Do you now?' he murmured, smiling a secret smile into her scented hair. Because that heartfelt capitulation somehow freed him from all the restraint he knew he should be exercising. A restraint he knew he should act on.

She was his secretary, for God's sake!

But suddenly that didn't matter. As she writhed against him unashamedly nothing mattered other than the urgent need to possess her. To see whether the body beneath matched up to all the tantalising promise which had been showcased by the scarlet dress. Which had driven him mad with desire all evening.

Deliberately, he circled his hips against hers and she gasped into his mouth as he slipped his hand into the bodice of her dress. He could feel her trembling anticipation as he took one breast into his palm and began to flick his thumb over the stiff, puckered nipple.

'Oh!' she cried out again, wriggling restlessly, her fingernails skating over his back and digging into his flesh through the silk shirt he wore. She was eager, he thought, his heart erratically missing a beat. *Very* eager. Once again, the voice of reason began to clamour in his head, demanding to be heard and to put a stop to this madness—but the needs of his body were more demanding still and he could hold back no longer as he began to ruck the slippery material up over her bottom.

It was a surprisingly firm bottom. Luxuriously, he smoothed his fingers over the high, tight globes—but his access to a still sweeter destination was impeded by the tights she wore.

Pulling his mouth away from hers, he looked down at her as he hooked a careless finger in the thick elastic of the waistband. 'I think we'd better take these off, don't you?' he questioned unsteadily.

Angie was so het up with need for him that she could hardly think, let alone speak. Her lips were dry and her heart was hammering but warning bells began to ring. Couldn't he just carry on what he was doing, which was giving her more pleasure than she'd ever thought it possible to feel? Strip her here without her having to give him permission to undress her. So that sex, if sex they were going to have, would be driven by passion rather than a cold-blooded discussion about it beforehand. And that way—driven by heated need rather than cool logic—he wouldn't get the chance to discover her relative inexperience until it was too late to stop.

And then she considered the reality of Riccardo removing her tights—the hold-everything-in tights which resembled cycling shorts and which she had bought deliberately to wear under the all-too-revealing outline of the thin silk dress. Because the last thing she had imagined was that *he* would be taking them off! Would he be disappointed when he saw what she was really like underneath—with a bit of a tummy, and hips about which the most flattering thing which had ever been said was that they were 'child-bearing'? How would she compare to the perfectly honed supermodels and actresses he usually went to bed with? Angie shivered with a mixture of dread and sheer excitement—because he was touching her bare skin.

Her lack of response to his question prompted him to rake his fingers through her hair, so that it spilled out all over his hands. Somehow the gesture made her feel curiously wanton—and so did the way he dipped his head to whisper his lips all the way along her shoulder blade.

'You are suddenly very quiet, *cara mia.*'

He made the silken words sound like poetry and the butterfly kiss which accompanied them was unbearably beautiful. Shuddering with pleasure, Angie swallowed down her self-doubts. She didn't care! She didn't care about support tights or the other women or the fact that they were in her grotty little apartment instead of the fancy places he was used to. All she cared about was Riccardo, the only man she ever *had* cared about, really—though she must never tell him that. Well, certainly not tonight!

She buried her lips in his ear. 'Yes, take them off,' she whispered.

Heatedly, Riccardo glanced around the room. Should he do it to her here? There was a small sofa and a floor covered by a rather tatty-looking carpet. If ever there was a room which was the antithesis of erotic, it was this one. 'Let's go to bed,' he said urgently. 'Come. Show me where it is.'

Lacing her fingers with his, Angie led him towards the bedroom—her heart racing with excitement and dread as she tried to see it through his eyes. But there was no time to wish that the place looked more welcoming or that the bed were bigger—because Riccardo was pulling her into his arms again and kissing her into sweet, soft submission once more before turning his attention to her clothes.

'Now…where was I?'

He slid the zip of her dress down so that it whispered into a scarlet pool by her feet. Next came her bra—he unclipped it with such frightening efficiency that it fluttered instantly to the floor. Only the tights slowed down his smooth progress—and it was with a bit of an effort that he peeled them off and flung them aside, his tongue trailing a moist path wherever her flesh was laid bare.

She gasped when he reached her belly, holding her breath as if scarcely able to believe that he was going to continue his erotic journey. And now he had buried his face in the soft fuzz of hair at the juncture of her thighs and she was shivering with what should have been embarrassment—that her boss should be performing such an intimate act on her. But Angie felt nothing except a wild and delirious excitement as he pushed her back onto the bed. Wasn't this what she'd spent the last four years dreaming about? She clawed at his shirt buttons, scrabbling to try to pop them open—and was it her imagination, or did she hear one bouncing to the ground?

'Ah, *cara. Lentamente*…slowly…' He was laughing softly now. Surprised—but very turned on by her impatience as he put his wallet, phone and keys on the bedside table. 'You must wait a little.'

But Angie didn't want to wait. She felt like someone who had just seen a rainbow—dazzled by its fragile beauty but aware that it could disappear in a moment. Because she loved this man. Hadn't she loved him for years—and wasn't this the natural conclusion to all those feelings? And the last thing she wanted was Riccardo having second thoughts and changing his mind about making love to her. If she was destined to spend her life alone—then at least she would have this one, glorious night to cherish in the lonely years ahead.

With a boldness she'd never before experienced she reached out and began to tug at the belt of his trousers and he groaned before removing her fingers.

'No!' he bit out.

'But—'

'I am too hot and hard to trust anyone but myself with my undressing,' he groaned as the zip rasped down and he kicked away the trousers before swiftly divesting himself of the rest of his clothes.

Then suddenly he was as naked as she and had joined her on the bed. The thin mattress dipped to the weight of an unaccustomed man beside her and Angie was glowingly aware of the long limbs which enfolded her and the dormant strength which shimmered beneath the muscular frame.

'Riccardo,' she whispered. Riccardo was in her bed and in her arms. She wanted to ask him whether this could really be happening to her. To him. To them. But she could find no words to frame such a question.

'Are you protected?' he demanded.

She shook her head and he said something terse in his native tongue before reaching for his wallet and withdrawing a condom.

'You want to put this on for me?' he questioned.

'No. You…you do it,' she said, suddenly shy—terrified that she wouldn't be able to do it. That her fingernails would snag it and he might think… But all her reservations dissolved as he started kissing her again—his beautiful mouth seeming to be on a mission to cover every centimetre of her skin.

She relaxed into it while the hunger built again—caught her up like a feather whirled into the eye of a storm—so that by the time Riccardo moved over her and into her, she gave a little cry.

Immediately, he stilled—his face suddenly a harsh mask of query. 'Please tell me,' he shuddered out, with an almighty effort, 'that you are not a virgin?'

Angie sensed some unknown emotion hovering in the atmosphere—something dark which threatened to destroy this fragile beauty. 'No,' she whispered. 'Of course I'm not.'

It was the *of course* which reminded him that all they were doing was taking their pleasure and Riccardo's lips twisted briefly as he began to move again. Tantalising her. Tormenting her. Driving her to the brink and then stopping. Demonstrating the control and technique for which he was renowned, until she begged him not to stop. And it was with that breathless little plea reverberating in his ears that at last Riccardo let go.

He felt her begin to shudder around him, collapsing against his chest with a little whimpering sound. And only then did he follow her—loving the sensation of spilling his seed into her, even while part of him resented it. Because that moment of letting go was the closest his powerful body ever came to weakness.

For a moment he lay there as sleep crept over him— the way it always did, no matter how much he tried to fight it. And this time he really *was* trying to fight it because there was no way he wanted to find himself in Angie's bed when the morning came. But his limbs felt heavy and lethargic and Riccardo knew that he was losing the battle as his eyelids became weighted down. Was this nature's way of keeping you close to the woman you'd made love to? he wondered drowsily.

Beside him, Angie held her breath until the steady rhythmical sound of his own breathing told her that he had fallen asleep—but still she didn't dare move, afraid of waking him, of shattering the spell. For surely some strange kind of magic had entered her life this evening? How else could she explain the fact that her beloved Riccardo was lying next to her, naked and contented after making love to her like…like…?

She swallowed. It had been the most wonderful experience of her life. Like everything she'd always known it could be. Like all the books said it could be—only she'd never really believed it before. She'd believed herself to be in love with him for years but the intimacy of actually making love with him had made that feeling increase a thousandfold. Her heart gave another skip—because she was daring to hope that it wasn't all one-sided. Because Riccardo couldn't have made love that way unless she actually *meant* something to him. Could he?

Carefully, she turned her head to look at him. Illuminated by the pale orange glow from the streetlight directly outside her window, he looked as if he had been fashioned in some precious metal—like those amazing statues you sometimes saw in museums. In this light his hair looked intensely black—as deep a colour as a moonless night—and the lush lashes which usually shaded the ebony eyes were now reposing in two dark feathered semi-circles on his cheeks. Never had she been given such a perfect opportunity to study him so closely and she drank in his beauty, noting how the high slash of his cheekbones cast perfect shadows on the golden skin.

Angie's heart missed a beat. So now what? She longed to reach out and touch him. To stroke his hair. To run her fingertips lovingly along the sculpted outline of his jaw. Perhaps to daringly continue their journey by tiptoeing them down the hard torso and further still—to his own dark tangle of hair. Should she…should she waken him erotically, as she had read that men liked to be awakened?

Or better to let him sleep? He had been under so much strain recently—quite apart from the ructions about his sister's wedding, he had been involved in several high-powered takeovers. And he was still probably jet-lagged. Wouldn't it be better to let him sleep—and in the morning, well, who knew?

She smiled. It was Saturday and neither of them had to work. *Then* she could wake him up with tiny kisses—as many as she liked—and after that she could make them coffee. Why, she might even be able to persuade him to stay in bed while she nipped down to the corner shop at the end of the road. They didn't sell the kind of high-end range of the market stuff he was used to—but they *did* stock croissants which tasted pretty good when you heated them up in the oven and served them with a dollop of cherry jam.

Angie gave a little sigh of contentment as she nestled down into the pillow. This morning she had been feeling close to despair and ready to start looking for a new job to get her away from the influence of her boss, and now…

Now?

She snuggled down even further. Now she felt as if the world had come alive with a powerful kind of magic.

What a difference a few hours could make.

CHAPTER FIVE

A MOTTLED ceiling swam into view and Riccardo quickly shut his eyes. But when he opened them again the ceiling was still there. And so was…so was…

So was he.

He held his breath for a moment as he realised that there was someone in the bed next to him and then he went cold when he remembered just who it was.

Angie!

Events from the previous day came flooding back in a dark and unwelcome tide. Giving her the dress. The Christmas party. Wine plus jet lag plus not very much supper. That damned dress! And then…then he had brought her home here and ravished her—and she had wholeheartedly let him.

His heart hammered in his chest as he lay there, dead still in the smallest bed he had slept in since childhood—until he could risk turning his head without waking her.

Without the dress she looked less like the siren of last

night and much more like the Angie he knew—though without her hair tied up. Her head was slumped back against the pillow, her face was flushed and the duvet had fallen down so that he could see one rosy little nipple.

Horror ran through him as his worst nightmare was realised.

He was lying naked in bed with his secretary!

For a moment he let his mind stray down tracks which would soon be out of bounds. The memory of her soft skin. Her unfeigned delight at his touch. The way she had kissed him—as if she had just discovered kissing for the first time. Resolutely he blocked the erotic recall.

Now what?

Gingerly, he began to edge one thigh towards the edge of the bed when he felt her stir beside him and instantly he stilled.

'Morning,' she murmured throatily.

Riccardo froze. She had that besotted note in her voice—a breathy kind of worship he recognised only too well. Women always used it after they'd had sex with him and there didn't seem to be a thing he could do about it. He turned to look down at her, steeling himself against that puppy-eyed look she was directing up at him. Because it wasn't her fault she was feeling that way; women were conditioned to react differently from men—everyone knew that. Give them a couple of orgasms and they started imagining all kinds of crazy notions. But with a little careful handling—those notions could be quickly consigned to the dust heap. And he needed to handle this very carefully indeed because he respected Angie.

As his secretary!

'Morning.' His smile was brief and perfunctory and—most important of all—non-committal. The kind of smile he might give if he was a couple of minutes late to a board-meeting. Leaning over, he planted a light kiss on the tip of her nose. It contained just the right amount of careless affection for her to be reassured that he didn't think too badly of her—but without giving her any false hope that this might be leading anywhere. Because it wasn't—and the sooner she understood that, the better. He pushed the duvet away and swung his long legs out of the bed, which hadn't seemed at all cramped last night—but which now felt like a tiny cage of a place.

Angie looked at him. 'You're not getting up?'

'I need the bathroom.'

Angie smiled. Of course he did. And how very intimate that sounded. 'It's down the—'

'I think I can probably find it by myself,' he offered drily.

He didn't seem at all fazed by his nakedness and Angie lay there and watched him leave the room— studying his muscular physique with greedy eyes. Those darkly powerful, hair-roughened legs contrasted with the paler globes of his buttocks where clearly he must have been sunbathing. She should have felt shy, anxious, insecure—but somehow she didn't. How could she, when he had made love to her so amazingly the night before—had made her feel like a real woman for the first time in her life? Riccardo was naked in her apartment and yet it seemed like the most natural thing in the world!

Wishing she'd had time to brush her teeth, she raked her fingers back through her tousled hair, plumped up the pillows and then arranged herself as decorously as possible against them, longing for him to kiss her again. But her heart sank in dismay when he walked back in the room and she saw that he was picking up a pair of silky boxer shorts which he'd dropped on the floor the night before and which he now looked as if he was about to put on.

She sat bolt upright, unable to keep the alarm from her voice. 'You're not…not…*going*, are you?'

'I have to.' He needed to. He needed to get his head straight and to extricate himself as quickly as possible to restore the right and normal order in his life. Because surely she could see that this episode—while enjoyable—was most definitely regrettable. And needed to be cut down and forgotten while it was still fresh enough to be killed off.

But sitting up like that had made the duvet tumble down to her waist and her hair to spill like wild honey all over her breasts—so that for one split second he forgot again that this was Angie. And that split second was enough. Enough to start the urgent tide of sexual desire from sweeping through him. He felt it instantly in the stiffening of his body and he saw from the widening of her eyes that she had noticed it, too.

'Do you really have to go?' she whispered, pride forgotten in her aching desire to be in his arms again.

Riccardo's mouth hardened along with the throb at his groin as he registered the provocation in her question and reminded himself that this wasn't some little innocent he was dealing with—but a sexually mature woman with desires of her own. Just like his. 'If you carry on staring at me with those big eyes and flaunting those amazing breasts of yours, then I may not be able to tear myself away, *mia bellezza.*'

Some unknown glint in his black eyes set off a tremor of apprehension whispering over her skin, but Angie resolutely pushed it away. She didn't want doubt—she wanted him. And he wanted her, too—she could see it in his eyes, even if his body wasn't making her so blatantly aware of that fact. So why not show him that she could be his equal in the bedroom, even if he was her boss in the boardroom?

'Who's asking you to?' she challenged softly.

A heartbeat of a pause. Then, dropping the shorts, he crossed the room and stood looking down at her—noting the invitation in her darkened eyes and parted lips. The rosy tips of her breasts were peaking beneath his gaze and suddenly he wanted nothing more than to put one sweet nub into his mouth and to lick and suck her there. Whipping back the duvet like a matador, he got on the bed and straddled her, gazing down on her with hungry intent, and then he caught her in his arms.

'Riccardo!' she gasped as he pushed her back down against the mattress.

'Riccardo!' he mocked, because in that instant he was angry—with her and with himself—for giving into temptation like this when he had already decided it was time to leave. Especially when the clarity which came with morning told him that this was simply prolonging the madness. But desire weakened a man. And no matter how much he knew he should just get up now and walk away—there didn't seem to be anything he could do to prevent his lips from brushing over her nipple. 'This is what you wanted, isn't it?' He felt her squirm beneath his touch as his hand moved down to capture her molten warmth. '*Isn't* it?'

'Y-yes. *Yes.*'

'This, too?'

Angie closed her eyes. 'Yes.'

'And this?' The movement of his fingers became more insistent. 'What about this?'

'You know I do!' Gasping again, she blocked the doubts which were now rearing their heads. Telling herself instead that it was glorious to be able to reacquaint herself with his body. To run the flats of her hands possessively over the hard flanks of his thighs. To have him kiss her again and then to feel his welcome weight as he slid on top of her, her body accommodating him as he entered her with such power, her heart thundering as he drove into her and again took her to that exquisite place and allowed her the slow, idyllic tumble down.

Afterwards, she trembled, reaching out her hand towards him—wanting intimacy of a different kind. And some kind of reassurance that they hadn't just done the most stupid thing in the world. 'Riccardo…'

A nerve flickered at the cheek she was stroking. 'Mmm?'

'That was…that was…'

He planted a quick kiss on top of her head and moved away from her. 'That was great sex, *piccola*—which probably should never have happened.'

At first she thought he was joking. Teasing her. But one look at the horribly familiar stubborn expression on his face told her that he was deadly serious—even if the fact that he was now climbing out of bed hadn't driven the point home with scalpel-sharp precision.

'You're *going*?'

This time the boxer shorts *did* make it onto his body—and were swiftly followed by the rest of his clothes—although he made a faint sound of disapproval when he slid the silk of his now completely crumpled shirt over his broad shoulders.

'I have to.'

He didn't say why and Angie began to sift through her memory to try to remember what appointments he had planned for today. But as far as she could recall, there was none.

She fixed a bright smile to her lips. 'You don't want any…breakfast, then?'

He thought of some awkward and protracted meal around that scruffy table of hers and only just suppressed a shudder. 'Tempting,' he murmured. 'But I'm afraid I don't have time.'

'Oh? Are you busy today, then?' she queried, though she hated herself for saying it. And even as she asked she was aware of a new and brittle note which had entered her voice. The old Angie would not have asked Riccardo a question so self-consciously. Nor have pinned quite so much hope on the answer.

Without answering, Riccardo walked back towards the sitting room in search of his jacket and he found it still hanging neatly over the back of the chair. He could hear the pad of bare feet and, in the middle of shrugging the jacket on, he looked up to find her watching him. She was tying the belt on some sort of silky kimono thing and he strove to find the most appreciative way of telling her that it had been a one-off, without actually having to spell it out. 'Listen, Angie—I had a great time—'

But Angie wasn't completely dense—and she had known Riccardo for long enough to recognise when he was giving someone the brush off. Hadn't she seen him doing it often enough during his business dealings? And so she cut him short—burying her hurt at the damning attitude he'd adopted with a crisp question of her own. 'What about Marco?'

'Marco?' he echoed blankly.

'Your driver and bodyguard. Remember? We left him sitting outside in the car last night.'

There was a pause. 'Marco can look after himself.'

Angie went over to peer out of the window, wondering how Riccardo's chauffeur-driven limousine would be received in the narrow and busy street in which she lived. 'He's gone!'

'Of course he's gone. He usually waits—'

Angie turned round, very slowly. 'Usually waits for *what*, Riccardo?'

Riccardo coiled his silken tie and shoved it into his jacket pocket. 'Nothing.'

'No, please—do tell me. Or maybe I can guess?' She felt the plummeting of her heart, the prickle of sweat between her breasts—but didn't she know that fears were better faced head on? It was not knowing which could eat away at you and destroy you with insecurity. Like all those times her parents had told the bewildered little girl that, no, nothing was wrong. And then it had turned out that Dad had been ill all along and by the time she found out just how bad it was, it was almost too late to say goodbye to him properly.

'Do you have an allotted time fixed for your nocturnal adventures?' she demanded. 'So that if you haven't reappeared by then, he knows you've struck lucky?'

He didn't flinch from her accusatory stare. 'Your words, Angie—not mine.'

She flushed. 'So I'm right.'

His mouth hardened. Was she hoping to make him

feel bad? Well, why the hell should he? She had been the one who had been practically begging him to take her. Who had been tantalising him all night long and crossing and uncrossing those milky thighs in his car. 'You think that this is the first time this particular scenario has taken place?' he drawled, and then his eyes flicked over her—at the swell of her beautiful breasts beneath the thin kimono. 'Not for either of us, I should imagine.'

Angie flinched. 'There's no need to make me sound like some sort of tramp!'

He shrugged. 'Again, your words, Angie. What is it that you say in England… "if the cap fits…"?'

She wanted to fly at him—to slap him hard around his arrogant olive face—but what good would that do? As if any woman could ever inflict pain on a man like Riccardo. Stung and angry, she opened her mouth to defend her honour and then shut it again, because there was no point. She could talk until she was blue in the face but it would be a complete waste of time. Riccardo would believe what he wanted to believe—the way he always did. Just as he believed that his sister should be grateful to be getting married to some aristocrat in what sounded like a loveless marriage!

Drawing back her shoulders, she proudly held her head up—striving for some kind of dignity when there seemed precious little else left. 'I think you'd better go now, don't you?'

Riccardo didn't move, his eyes narrowing as he registered her anger, trying to work out the best way to calm the situation down. Because although what had happened should never have happened—it wasn't worth making a big deal out of. It certainly wasn't worth jeopardising their perfect working relationship for. And Angie wouldn't want to throw away a well-paid job simply because they'd both got a little carried away after a few drinks. Give her a couple of days and she'd probably feel secretly relieved that he had seen sense. He tried to defuse the tension with a rare and indulgent smile. 'Look, let's just forget this ever happened, shall we?' he suggested easily. 'Let's go back to the way it was before.'

Did he really and truly think it was that simple? Silently, Angie counted to ten. If only he knew how close she was to picking up last night's mug of cold coffee and tipping it all over his arrogant black head. But if she demonstrated her anger or her hurt—then wouldn't that make him think that she *cared*? And she didn't. Not any more. For how could she care about a man who had a lump of stone for a heart? Who could take her to heaven and back in his arms and then leave her feeling like some cheap little tramp in the morning?

'Just *go*,' she repeated, marching to the front door and averting her eyes as she held it open for him, afraid that he would see the tears of shame and humiliation which were threatening to spill from her eyes.

CHAPTER SIX

'YOU'RE not eating very much, Angie.'

'I'm not that hungry, Mum.'

'Oh, don't give me that, darling. It *is* Christmas day. Go on—have some more!'

Angie's smile didn't slip as she obediently speared a sprout and began chewing it even though she felt as if the effort might choke her. But then it had been like that ever since she'd woken up that morning and eyed the few presents under the tree with a dutiful rather than enthusiastic eye. If the truth were known, she'd rather have put her head back under the duvet and stayed in bed all day than have to go through the charade of celebrating!

Yet her Christmas probably looked picture-perfect from the outside—with snow tumbling prettily down over the houses in the village where her mother lived and every shiny front door decked with a bright wreath of holly. You could have painted the scene and stuck it on the front of a Christmas card and people would have cooed over it.

There had been a traditional service in the tiny church, chatting to people she'd known since she'd been a little girl and then trudging back through the silent white lanes to open their presents. But her mother always found this particular holiday difficult and Angie had been aware of a terrible dull ache which had nothing to do with it being the anniversary of her father's death. Her sister's current marital woes weren't helping matters any either.

Phone calls had been arriving with scary regularity from Australia. Angie had worried how on earth her sister was going to pay for them all with a costly divorce pending—and she wasn't even sure how useful they were, since they consisted mainly of Sally sobbing and saying how unhappy she was with the 'Aussie idiot'.

'Believe me, Angie,' she had sniffed. 'There's a lot to be said for the single life!'

Not from where Angie was sitting. Today, she felt like the loneliest person on the planet—an uncomfortable feeling only sharpened by her regret at having so recklessly gone to bed with Riccardo.

Riccardo. Angie swallowed down the last of the sprout and tried not to feel sick. It didn't matter what she did or said—nor how much she tried to fill her waking hours with mundane tasks which would occupy her mind—her thoughts stubbornly kept coming back to the arrogant Italian.

The glow of physical pleasure had faded quickly—helped by the knowledge that he regretted the sex had ever happened. His hasty retreat from her apartment had left her feeling abandoned and foolish. And she had quickly realised that her long-cherished dream of ending up in the arms of her boss hadn't turned out as she'd expected.

Because Riccardo didn't want her. Not in any way which didn't involve fielding his phone-calls or typing his letters. He didn't even desire her enough to want to repeat the sex on a different occasion—why, he'd left so fast that morning that she hadn't seen him for dust. And if she'd been harbouring some small hope that he might have had second thoughts—that he might have rung her up to apologise for his abruptness and to ask to see her again outside work—well, that hope too had been crushed. There had been nothing but a deafening kind of silence from Signor Castellari.

And then, of course, there was the bigger picture. Like, what the hell was she going to do when she got back to work after the holiday was over? Act as if it had never happened? Primly place his coffee on the desk in front of him while trying not to remember the way that he had pushed her hair back from her face and then lowered his head to kiss her? Or remember the way that his tongue had trickled its way over an extremely intimate part of her anatomy? Her cheeks flushing with remorse, Angie bit her lip. There was no way she was going to be able to remain there, that much was certain. Before Christmas she had been aware that she couldn't stay working for Riccardo for ever—but that vague wish had now become an absolute necessity.

As soon as she got back to London, she would start applying for a new job.

'Are you all right, dear?'

Her mother's voice broke into her silent deliberations and Angie quickly put her fork down.

'Yes, Mum—I'm fine.'

'You've been distracted since you arrived. Nothing's *wrong*, is it, Angelina?'

Angie managed a weak smile. 'No, of course not. Nothing's wrong.' Because what woman in the world could confide to her mother that she had broken the cardinal rules of advancement in the workplace? Never mix business with pleasure. Never fall for a man who is light years out of your league. And never end up in bed with the boss after the Christmas party.

'And how's that nice boss of yours?'

Could mothers mind-read? 'Oh, he's…he's fine. Successful as ever.'

'So I keep reading in the newspapers,' murmured her mother approvingly. 'You were so *lucky* the way he plucked you out of the typing pool like that!'

Angie only just stopped herself from cringing at her mother's choice of words—but, come to think of it, didn't she used to feel exactly the same way about her rapid promotion? As if Riccardo were some kind of knight in shining armour, galloping into the office and carrying her away on his white charger. Back then, in her eyes, her boss could do no wrong—no matter how irascible he could be. In a way, she had been stuck in a groove of adoring him—her mind still fixed in the same mode it had been when he'd 'rescued' her.

Except he hadn't done anything of the sort. All he had done was recognise that he'd found a woman who would completely submerge her life in his. Who would put up with just about anything he cared to throw at her. Long, thankless hours spent helping him meet some deadline or other—just for the occasional heart-fluttering smile or glinty-eyed look he threw across the office.

And just because he'd done the unthinkable—events had taken an unexpected turn. If he hadn't bought her the kind of dress she would never normally have looked at, then she would never have been transformed into someone else. Someone who had taken a night off from being Angie—so that Riccardo hadn't treated her like Angie at all. He'd treated her like a woman he'd just been tantalised by. He'd taken her to bed and made her discover just how wonderful a man could make you feel. And just because she had woken up the next morning in a smitten state and wondering if perhaps they had some kind of future together didn't mean that he felt the same way.

On the contrary. He wanted to erase the woman in the red dress from his mind and replace her with the old, familiar version of herself—the dull one that he scarcely noticed. Angie didn't know whether that was possible—and, more importantly, she had to ask herself whether she wanted it, even if it was. Could you possibly go back to the life you'd been living after an event like that?

'So what's he doing for Christmas?' asked her mother brightly.

Angie shrugged. 'Same as he always does. Spending it with his family in Tuscany.'

'In the castle?'

'Yes, Mum—in the castle. They're all getting ready for a wedding—his sister's getting married to a Duke in the new year.'

'A *Duke*?'

'Well, they call him a *Duca* but it means the same thing.'

'Oh, Angelina,' sighed her mother. 'It sounds just like a fairy tale.'

Yes, it did, thought Angie grimly. But it was as illusionary as any other fairy tale—with all those dark undercurrents swirling around beneath the supposedly perfect surface.

Angie felt a new restlessness as she mentally psyched herself up to going back to work, staring at her bland image in the mirror and trying hard not to remember how different she'd looked in the bright party dress. For the first time in her life she had seen how clothes could make you blossom. Could make a man—even a man as gorgeous as Riccardo—look at you with naked desire in his eyes.

She might have hung the scarlet dress at the back of her wardrobe, vowing never to wear it again—but she realised that everything else she owned made her look and feel like a piece of wallpaper. She blended in so that nobody noticed her; she always had. But suddenly the prospect of continuing down that road terrified her.

She was scared that she would become completely invisible—inside and out. That if she wasn't careful, she would let the destruction of her dreams slide her into a dark place from which she might not emerge. And she wasn't going to live like that. Not any more.

Her clothes were expensive and she could never afford to replace her wardrobe overnight—especially not with the cheap kind of clothes which didn't really suit her—but surely she could brighten things up with a few carefully chosen accessories bought in the post-Christmas sales?

She found herself in a huge department store on Oxford Street, drifting her fingertips through a filmy selection of shawls. Holding a vivid red one next to her face and deciding that perhaps vibrant colours brought out her colouring in a way that her usual camel or taupe didn't.

She bought a wide brown leather belt which cinched in her waist and made it look impossibly small—and another in glossy black patent. And a rich, emerald velvet scarf which emphasised the green flecks in her hazel eyes. New, squashy brown leather boots too—and a pair of high black court shoes. Brightly coloured beads cost very little, but gave a dress an entirely new appearance—or so the helpful girl on the jewellery stand told her. And when she went to her new job she wouldn't be classified by her fellow workers as a bland, boring person whom nobody noticed. They would think of her as bright, bouncy Angie who wore a clutch of plastic bangles which clanked as she moved.

But the most daring thing of all she saved until last—walking into the hairdresser's with a defiant expression on her face and letting her sand-coloured hair spill all over her shoulders.

'Can you just cut it off?' she asked.

'Anything particular in mind?' asked the assistant.

'Something really flattering,' said Angie, colouring slightly. 'But nothing too wild.'

It seemed to Angie that her new haircut and her new boots and belt became more about trying to update her image without losing her essential personality—but they also felt like a shield she could hide behind. And if she felt brittle on the inside as she travelled into work after the Christmas break—she knew that from the outside she looked newly bright and breezy.

The snow had melted into a thick grey slush but the man who owned the coffee shop next door lifted her spirits, telling her she was the best thing he'd seen all year.

'Ah, but that's because it's only the second of January!' She smiled, though if she'd been paying more attention she might have noticed the dark figure who had paused momentarily outside the plate-glass window.

But despite her determination not to slink into work as if she were ashamed of herself, Angie's heart was still beating quickly as she walked into the office carrying her blueberry muffin. With a nervous repetition which bordered on hysteria, she silently told herself that since

Riccardo didn't have a meeting until lunch-time, he probably wouldn't be in the office until later.

But he was.

Sitting at his desk, his chair pushed back and his long legs stretched out in front of him, he was flicking through a sheaf of papers and he glanced up as she walked in.

And frowned.

Angie hung her coat up as she met his gaze, praying that her own face held just the right amount of friendly interest which you might direct at your boss if the last time you'd seen him he had just been putting his clothes back on. But his face was looking distinctly stony and her heart sank.

'Happy new year!' she said, nervous words tumbling out of her mouth. 'How was Tuscany? Busy, I expect. Not long now until the wedding.'

He completely ignored her question and her babbled statements, the black eyes flicking over her with an incredulous light in their ebony depths. And when he spoke, his voice was silky—a tone she'd never heard before and didn't quite recognise. 'Well, well, well. And what, pray, is this?'

Steadily, she regarded him—praying that her calm face didn't betray a trace of the heart-thumping excitement she felt at being alone with him again. Because she didn't want to feel heart-thumping excitement. She wanted nothing more than neutrality to get her through the days until she could slap her resignation letter on his desk and walk away without a backward glance.

'What is *what*?' she questioned brightly even though her heart was slamming against her ribcage.

Riccardo flicked her another cool glance. He had psyched himself up for a very different encounter. Had been expecting—and dreading—Angie to creep into the office with red-rimmed eyes. For her to sulk and pointedly give him the cold shoulder. For cups of coffee to be slammed down in front of him. And that the memories of that unbelievably erotic night would fade with every glance he cast over her drab figure. Except that she wasn't looking in the slightest bit drab. He frowned again.

What the hell had changed? He was sure the plain woollen dress she wore wasn't new and yet the garment seemed to have undergone a dramatic transformation. Was it the tight belt which was drawing his attention to the narrow curve of her waist and the tempting swell of her breasts? Or just the fact that he now knew what treasures the dress concealed? He felt his throat constrict. 'You've…you've had your hair cut,' he said suddenly.

He'd noticed! Angie felt a shaft of pleasure pierce her—until she forced herself to get real. Don't be so pathetic. He's noticed that at long last you've changed your hairstyle—big deal. Nevertheless, her fingertips touched the newly shorn locks.

'That's right. Do you…do you like it?' The question came out before she could stop it—did it sound like the desperate query of a discarded lover keen to reappraise herself in the eyes of the man who had walked away?

Riccardo's gaze flicked over her. Unfortunately, the question required him to continue looking at her, and looking at her was the last thing he wanted. Or rather, it was. It was just that looking at her made him remember the pink and cream softness of her body and the way she had cried out when he had entered her.

Today she didn't look remotely pink. Or soft. She looked glossy, and sleek. Like some pampered little pussy-cat who was longing to be stroked.

With an effort, he forced his mind away from the pert thrust of her breasts and up to the shiny new haircut. Did he like it? It was difficult to judge because his head was now full of conflicting images which were jangling for his attention. Angie with her hair scraped back from her face in its usual stark, utilitarian style. Angie with her hair spread out all over the pillow. And now Angie with her hair all feathered around her chin and showcasing a remarkably long and slender neck. He gave a non-committal shrug. 'It's okay.'

Suddenly Angie understood the meaning of the expression being damned with faint praise. So stop seeking it, she told herself fiercely. Act like you'd normally act—the way you used to before you spent the night with him. The trouble was although she could remember how—she wasn't sure whether she was going to be able to accomplish it. She had been in love with him for so long, but had become an expert at hiding her feelings for him behind the easy working relationship they'd forged. But now it felt all skewed. Odd.

Now she knew the reality of Riccardo as a lover and it was the memories of *that* which dominated her thoughts. For how could you possibly keep your mind on his latest financial acquisition when you kept being reminded of the way his lips had whispered with a featherlight touch across your bare belly?

Remember how callous he was the morning after you slept with him, she told herself. Remember how your stupid heart was welling up with love for him and he took those feelings and crushed them beneath the heel of his arrogant Italian shoe.

'I'm just going to make some coffee,' she said.

'I don't want a cup of coffee.'

'Well, I do.' Tearing her eyes away from his piercing black gaze, she clattered around with the sophisticated coffee machine he'd insisted on installing when he'd first arrived—which produced coffee to rival the stuff served in the shop next door. But it wasn't until she'd completed the task and put the cup on her desk that she realised he was still looking at her. And that there was no way she was going to be able to munch her way through the skinny blueberry muffin she'd brought in for breakfast. But neither could she ignore the accusatory stare which was lancing through her.

'Is something wrong, Riccardo?'

'I just wondered why you'd come to work looking as if you were going straight out to a party.'

Angie feigned outrage at the acid remark, though secretly she was pleased; more than pleased. So he'd noticed her clothes, had he? Good. And he disapproved of them, did he? Even better.

'I don't think that's an accurate assessment of a simple woollen dress you've seen many times before, do you?' she asked coolly.

Riccardo gave what sounded uncomfortably like a growl—though the sound wasn't nearly as uncomfortable as the sudden heavy aching at his groin. He was overreacting and it was time to stop it. He should be grateful that she'd had the sense not to play up—or want to talk about what had happened after the Christmas party. His mouth hardened. Even though her reasons for sharpening up her wardrobe were quite clear. Women could be so transparent. She thought he'd go right over there and rip it off, didn't she? Thought he'd be laying her over the desk, and pulling down her...

'Is something wrong, Riccardo?'

Uncomfortably, he snapped out of his erotic daydream. 'Why?'

'You'd just gone a rather peculiar colour, that's all.'

His black eyes seared through her. Was she daring to *taunt* him? 'Make me a coffee!' he ordered.

'But you just said—'

'I don't care what I *said*, Angie—just make me a coffee, will you—since that's one of the things I pay you to do!'

Not for much longer, she thought furiously as she got up and walked over to the coffee machine.

She could feel his eyes burning into her as she clattered around and tried to stop her fingers from shaking.

But when she placed the cup carefully in front of him, his hand snaked out to capture her wrist.

'So are you enjoying a flirtation with that man?' he demanded.

Pulse rocketing in instant response to his touch, she stared at him incredulously. As if she could even *look* at another man! '*Which* man?'

'The one who owns the sandwich shop next door.'

For a moment she almost laughed until she realised that he was deadly serious. 'Don't be so absurd, Riccardo.'

His fingers tightened around her wrist. 'But I saw you on my way into the office. Fluttering your eyelashes at him. Wiggling your hips in the way a woman does when she is aware of her own sexual power.'

And despite the ludicrous nature of his accusation, Angie could feel the urgent escalation of her heart and the now thready flutter of her pulse beneath his fingers. Could he feel it, too? she wondered. Was he as affected by her touch as she was by his? Quickly, she snatched her hand away—terrified at how quickly that brief, almost contemptuous contact could still make her melt with longing. 'You're being ridiculous!'

'You think so? Yet I recognise all too well the signs of desire in a man.' His gaze was steady, but inside he was angry. With himself, more than anyone—because she seemed to be showing a remarkable sangfroid he was far from feeling. He wanted to storm round to the other side of his desk and kiss her until she begged him to take her. He wanted to lose himself in her sweet softness one more time… Instead, he glared at her. 'Who knows? Perhaps I am not the only recipient of your undeniably sweet favours.'

Angie stared at him in disbelief. And yet—could she blame him for making such an accusation? Hadn't she just fallen into bed with him, with nothing in the way of real wooing? He wasn't to know that there had only ever been one lover in her life, and that had been a bit of a disaster. 'You…really…really think *that*, Riccardo?'

He didn't know what to think; the rule-book seemed to have been torn up and flung out of the window during that inexplicably erotic night with her. And he was behaving in a way which was completely out of character. As if he cared *what* she did!

He shrugged. 'It is none of my business what you do or who you associate with. You must have all the boyfriends you wish. You are a free agent.' There was a pause. 'As am I.'

And this hurt almost as much as anything else he had said—his precise words making it patently clear that their one night really *had* been one night. Well, she would not react. He would never know how much she cared for him. How much she *had* cared for him, she corrected herself silently.

'I know that, Riccardo. And if you don't mind—I'd prefer not to discuss what happened before Christmas. I thought we'd already decided that.' Or rather, he had decided it. She gave him a thin smile. 'It was unfortunate, yes—a mistake which should never be repeated—so the sooner it's forgotten, the better. Don't you agree?'

For a moment, he was completely taken aback. That was supposed to be *his* line. *He* was the one who erected boundaries in his relationships and other people were the ones who fell in with his wishes. And she was daring to call it a *mistake*? *A mistake to have spent the night in the arms of Riccardo Castellari!* For a moment he was tempted to go round there and take her in his arms and kiss her and *then* let her tell him it was a mistake. As if she could! But he did not need to prove his sexual power to anyone—least of all to himself. And wasn't it easier this way? With Angie taking the whole episode in her stride—even if it *was* only an act and secretly she was longing for his kiss once more?

'It's forgotten. It is of no consequence,' he drawled, with a careless shrug. 'Now get me all the paperwork on the Posara account, would you? And after that I'd like you to organise a conference call with Zurich about the Close merger. Oh, and can you sort out a fitting for the suit I'm wearing to my sister's wedding?'

'My pleasure,' she answered tightly as she walked over towards the filing cabinet.

For the rest of the day, they barely spoke—except when it was impossible not to—and Angie buried herself in her work, staying on late in the office after Riccardo had departed to get ready for some fancy black-tie dinner which was taking place at Somerset House, with its beautiful ice rink and views of the river.

Was he taking some other woman to it? she wondered jealously as sat poring over the job advertisements. Of course he was! As if a man like Riccardo Castellari would ever go to a do like that on his own.

She thought of the long journey home and the cold little apartment which awaited her. The day she'd just spent—trying her best to be professional but unable to ignore the tension which had been sizzling across the office between her and Riccardo, no matter how much they'd both kept their distance, circling round each other like two wary animals.

How could she bear to exist in that kind of atmosphere—while his imposing presence mocked her with the pleasures he had given her, which were destined never to be repeated? The simple answer was that she couldn't.

Staring at the blank screen, Angie began composing a letter of application with a grim new determination.

CHAPTER SEVEN

'WOULD you mind stepping into the office for a moment, Angie?'

Angie looked up to see the unfamiliar sight of her boss standing at the door of the staffroom—a place he rarely visited—and instantly there was a buzz of conversation as every single woman in the room sat up straight. She had been sitting chatting to Alicia because the rain was lashing down too hard to even think of going outside during her lunch-hour and she wasn't expecting Riccardo back in the office until later on. His black hair was spattered with rain and so was his dark cashmere coat. And he had a look of pure, dark fury on his face that set off warning bells deep inside her.

She gave him a slightly uneasy smile—and gestured to her half-eaten sandwich. 'Sure. Do you mind if I just—?'

'Why don't you bring it with you?' he snapped. 'I want to talk to you *now*.'

Angie flushed as she stood up, picking up the rest of her lunch and dropping it in the bin, trying to ignore the interested sympathy in Alicia's eyes and the exchanged glances of the other secretaries. It was humiliating to be spoken to like that—especially in front of other people. And especially after she'd had to field so many embarrassing questions about what it had been like to have been given a lift home in Riccardo's chauffeur-driven car after the Christmas party.

Ever since the new year, she had been given a crash-course in evasion—she couldn't bear to think of it as lying. But what else could she do other than giving fudging, half-truth replies to an impressionable young girl like Alicia? Coming out and admitting that she'd spent a passionate night with the boss was hardly portraying herself as the ideal role model to one of the junior staff, was it?

She followed Riccardo out of the staffroom, trying to keep up with his determined stride, but his long legs meant that he far outpaced her.

'Is something wrong?' she puffed, when finally they reached his penthouse office.

'Shut the door,' he said ominously.

Angie swallowed. 'Riccardo—'

'I said, shut the door.'

Hands trembling, she obeyed him, looking up at him with some inexplicable feeling of dread building inside her as he hung up his rain-spattered coat. 'Has something happened?' she questioned.

Black eyes flicked over her. At the way the fabric of her dress clung to her breasts. 'Damned right it has.'

Her brow creased with anxiety. 'Nothing to do with the family, I hope.'

He glared down at her. Wasn't that just like Angie to worry about someone else? But now he found himself wondering how much of her supposedly soft nature had just been an act—concealing a person he was fast discovering he didn't know at all. And maybe he didn't. Because, if Riccardo was being honest, hadn't the very macho side of his nature been slightly appalled at the ease with which Angie had switched from secretary to lover?

Hadn't he put her in the category of women who would have been appalled that he should have made a pass at her—and primly shown him the door instead of welcoming him into her body with a passionate zeal which had rocked him. Furious with himself for a train of thoughts which was having predictable consequences on his body, he glared at her. 'Don't try and change the subject!' he bit out.

'I wasn't.'

'Tell me, Angie,' he said, in a voice of soft danger, 'were you ever going to get around to telling me that you're planning on leaving?'

Heart scudding fast with panic, Angie stared at him, her mind working overtime. Yes, she'd sent off several job applications—but she hadn't heard a whisper back from any of them. There certainly hadn't been any intimation that anybody was currently taking up references about her suitability for any post. Why, she hadn't even been shortlisted for any interviews!

'Well, I'm *not* leaving—strictly speaking,' she said. 'I'm *thinking* about leaving and I've applied for a few jobs, but I haven't got anything else to go to. I haven't even been for an interview yet.'

'You didn't think,' breathed Riccardo, trying to dampen down his anger—and his growing feeling of frustration, 'that it might be polite to have given me some kind of warning about your plans—especially in view of the fact that you've worked for me for so long? Or didn't you think I was owed that kind of courtesy?'

For a moment Angie had to struggle with the temptation to fling his accusation back in his face. She wondered what he'd say if she dared challenge *him*. Had he shown *her* anything in the way of courtesy when he'd hightailed it out of her apartment—looking as if she'd tainted him?

'I *was* going to tell you!'

'When?'

'I was waiting to find the right time.' She regarded him, knowing that when Riccardo was in this kind of spiky mood it was best to tread carefully. 'How…how did you find out?'

'How?' He made an angry little noise, midway between a laugh and a snort. 'Why, when one of my biggest rivals came up to me at a fancy dinner last night and asked me whether he thought he'd be in with a chance of getting his hands on the best secretary in the business.'

Angie flushed with pleasure. 'But isn't that a kind of compliment?' she asked. 'To you as well as to me?'

'And how precisely do you work that out?' he questioned silkily, wondering why her cheeks had gone so pink. Was there something else she wasn't telling him? Had she enjoyed the chauffeur-driven ride home more than she'd let on? So much that she had seen a glimpse of a world she would like to inhabit—because wasn't that what women did when they caught that first heady whiff of real wealth?

Had she perhaps reconciled herself to the fact that he knew her far too well to ever contemplate taking her as his lover? But that maybe with her new and inexplicable brand of sexuality—which had been kick-started by the red dress—she might now find a more receptive audience in another wealthy man. Did that explain the new haircut—and the way she seemed to have sexed-up her wardrobe? His mouth hardened. 'How is it flattering to me for everyone in the business world to be aware that you're leaving—except for me? You know that at this end of the corporate world good secretaries are like gold dust!'

'Exactly!' said Angie. 'It's a reflected compliment. Don't you see? He rates *me* and so therefore he is applauding *your* judgement!'

'My ego isn't so diminished that I need my worth to be reflected by my staff,' came the cutting retort.

'No, I suppose not.'

'It was the "getting his hands" on you that made me rather concerned for your welfare and concerned about something else, too,' he responded coolly. There was a pause as the black eyes drifted over her. 'Have you been gossiping about our night together, Angie?'

Her colour heightened as the hateful sting behind his words pricked at her skin. 'Of *course* I haven't!' she retorted.

'Sure?' he questioned mockingly. 'You haven't been boasting to the typing pool that you managed to get your clutches in the boss and that he's a red-hot lover? Word gets around, you know—especially over something as sensational as that.'

That did it. Angie's temper boiled over. Despite knowing that it was probably the most foolish response in the world, her indignation was so intense that she just couldn't help herself.

'You bastard!' she shot at him, her hand flying to his face, hating him for making her feel like some gossipy little nobody who for one night only had bagged the big prize. 'You think you're so great, do you?'

But his reaction was lightning-sharp and he instantly deflected her intended strike with a swift and effortless capture—his hand wrapping around her tiny wrist as he hauled her up close to him. And that was dangerous. More than dangerous. She could feel the sheer heat which was emanating from his powerful body and she could feel its hard contours, too.

'My greatness was never in any doubt,' he hissed. 'But don't you think you've made me look a fool?'

'Is that all you care about, you arrogant pig—your reputation?'

He gave a low laugh, knowing that with her care-lessly insulting words she had sealed her fate. Their professional relationship was to all intents and purposes over—and thus there was no longer any need to deny himself what he wanted. What she wanted too, judging from the way her lips trembled and her eyes had widened into black pools he could have dived into. 'No, *piccola*, that's just where you're wrong,' he mocked softly. 'You see, right now there are more immediate concerns on my mind than my professional reputation.'

And with that he drove his mouth down on hers in a hard, almost punishing kiss.

Angie tried to fight it. Tried to fight herself—but within seconds she knew that it was a battle she was destined to lose. Anger made her frantic and desire made her weak. And despite everything—Riccardo made her feel alive. *Alive.*

'Riccardo,' she breathed against his seeking lips as she caught onto his broad shoulders as if they were a lifeline. As if he were the only solid object in her world and she needed to hold onto him. As if she needed to say his name aloud again to convince herself that he was real. 'Oh, Riccardo.'

The unashamed emotion in her voice struck him in a way he had not expected and he went up in flames. He had spent the entire holiday season see-sawing between calming the pre-wedding nerves of his sister and re-membering that stolen night with Angie. As the days had ticked away he had wondered whether it really could have happened. Whether he really could have *allowed* it to happen. And now, feeling her soft and supple body in his arms once more, he could see exactly how.

Lust—pure, potent and powerful—pumped through his veins like life-blood as his hand grasped a cashmere-covered breast and he felt it peak against the fine wool.

'Oh,' she breathed instantly, melting into his hard body—her fingers wrapping themselves around his neck, wanting him closer still. She made no protest when he pushed her to the floor, nor when he began to smooth his hands down the sides of her body—as if he were reacquainting himself with her, by touch alone. Instead, she felt her body rearing towards his—as if it had been conditioned to put as little space between the two of them as possible.

His lips moved to her neck. 'You're driving me crazy—do you know that?'

'S-snap,' she managed, through bone-dry lips.

He tried to tell himself that he shouldn't be doing this—but hard on the heels of that one intrusive thought came another. Could he strip her bare? Was there time to have her lying naked on the floor of his office—her limbs splayed out with indolent abandon—so that he could feast his eyes on her pink and white softness while he made love to her one more blissful time?

No. This whole scenario was crazy enough—but that would be sheer madness. And what if someone came in? Urgently, Riccardo began to ruck up her dress. Nobody would dare to come in—not without knocking first. And in the meantime, he couldn't wait any longer.

FREE BOOKS OFFER

To get you started, we'll send you
2 FREE books and a FREE gift

There's no catch, everything is **FREE**

Accepting your 2 **FREE** books and **FREE** mystery gift places you under no obligation to buy anything.

Be part of the Mills & Boon® Book Club™ and receive your favourite Series books up to 2 months before they are in the shops and delivered straight to your door. Plus, enjoy a wide range of **EXCLUSIVE** benefits!

- Best new women's fiction – delivered right to your door with FREE P&P
- Avoid disappointment – get your books up to 2 months before they are in the shops
- No contract – no obligation to buy

We hope that after receiving your free books you'll want to remain a member. But the choice is yours. So why not give us a go? You'll be glad you did!

Visit **millsandboon.co.uk** to stay up to date with offers and to sign-up for our newsletter

2 **FREE** books and a **FREE** gift

P9JI9

Mrs/Miss/Ms/Mr   Initials

BLOCK CAPITALS PLEASE

Surname

Address

Postcode

Email

MILLS & BOON®
Pure reading pleasure

NO STAMP
NEEDED!

MILLS & BOON®
Book Club

FREE BOOK OFFER
FREEPOST NAT 10298
RICHMOND
TW9 1BR

NO STAMP
NECESSARY
IF POSTED IN
THE U.K. OR N.I.

Angie shuddered as his lips moved from her neck to her jaw and then began to graze at her mouth—and as she responded hungrily to that tantalising, teasing kiss she could feel him begin to peel off her tights.

'Should…should we be doing this?' she managed.

'Sì,' he ground out, tossing the tights away and whispering his fingertip inside her panties so that she bucked.

'Oh.'

'Unzip me,' he demanded unsteadily.

With infinite trembling care, Angie complied—dealing with the soft leather belt with dextrous skill and then carefully sliding down the zip and hearing him bite out his pleasure as she freed him. She had never made love like this before—with a frantic disregard for anything other than the urgent need to join together. So that clothes were merely a barrier to be removed as swiftly and as efficiently as possible.

'Please, Riccardo,' she begged as he began to slide her panties down over her knees.

'Please what?' he taunted, but he was having trouble putting on the condom, he was so aroused.

Her head fell back. 'I'm not going to beg you,' she slurred.

'I'll stop then, shall I?' he demanded silkily.

Her eyes trembled open to find that the mocking challenge of his words was not matched by the opaque look of hunger in his black eyes   and suddenly Angie didn't care about games, or power. All she cared about was him; but then she always had.

'No, don't stop,' she whispered, and the words seemed to come straight from her heart. 'Just make love to me.'

If he fundamentally disagreed with her choice of words—that there was little of love in this swift coupling—he was in no fit state to be able to articulate it. All he could do was thrust into her—as if driven by a force far stronger than his own will, or sense of reason. And all he could feel was her melting, welcoming tightness and the way she clung to him. The little sounds she made before he was forced to kiss silent her gasping orgasm—until his own made the world retreat, like the distant sound of people playing on the shoreline when you were swimming far out to sea.

It seemed to take for ever before he felt consciousness return—though it was probably only minutes—and for a moment Riccardo just registered all the sensations which were bathing his body in a warm glow. The feel of her warm breath fanning contentedly against his neck in small, even sighs. Her arms wrapped tightly around his back as if she never wanted to let him go. And her fading waves of pleasure pulsating softly against his manhood.

He felt her wriggle contentedly—and, with a reluctance which surprised him, slowly began to disentangle himself. 'You'd better straighten your clothing,' he said abruptly.

His harsh words shattered the dreamy thoughts she'd been having and Angie opened her eyes. If she had been hoping for passionate words to end such a passionate interlude, then it seemed she was to be badly disappointed. And there she had been—stupidly fantasising that Riccardo might actually care about her. How wrong could she be? As if a proud and patrician man could ever care about a woman who let him take her on the office floor with such careless abandon. Slowly, she sat up—still feeling dizzy and now slightly empty as she grabbed at her discarded tights, her cheeks flaming with shame.

'I need…to freshen up,' she said and on bare feet she walked unsteadily over to the bathroom which stood at the far end of the office suite. Once inside, she concentrated fiercely on pulling herself together—glad that Riccardo's European sensibilities meant that he'd insisted on installing a bidet. But the act of touching herself where he had so recently touched her somehow made her feel more decadent still—and hot on the evocative memories of how he'd made her react came the tumbling feelings of insecurity.

Smelling now of spicy fragrant soap, she risked a look in the mirror—splashing cold water over her heated cheeks and raking her fingers back through the new haircut in an attempt to restore some order. But no sense of order could dampen down the tumult of her thoughts.

She half wondered if Riccardo might not have taken himself from the office during her absence—because wouldn't that be easier for both of them? If he went away and then came back later as if nothing had happened. To pretend that such an angry and erotic encounter had never taken place. But he had not. He was still there—though thank heavens he had moved from the floor and had straightened his own clothes. Now he was leaning back against the giant desk, looking like a king surveying one of his lowly subjects as she walked back into the office with her head held determinedly high.

But she had just had sex with him, for heaven's sake—the most unbelievably exciting sex she could have imagined. Sex that he had instigated and that she, so completely transfixed by him, had joyously participated in. So she was not going to act as if nothing had happened. It had—and she needed to know where she stood.

She drew in a deep breath. 'So now what, Riccardo?'

From between narrowed eyes he regarded her. Or rather, he regarded the curve of her bottom since she was in the process of retrieving her shoes and putting them back on. And then she straightened up—and it was…amazing. He swallowed. Apart from the faint flush of pink to her cheeks and the extra-bright glitter to her eyes you wouldn't think she had just been doing anything more taxing than taking dictation. And the memory of just how enthusiastically she had writhed beneath him made him begin to grow hard again. How could this damned mouse of a woman make him feel so horny?

His black eyes glittered. 'You're applying for other jobs. You don't want to work for me any more.'

It was more a question of what she needed, rather than what she *wanted*. Because what she wanted from Riccardo he would never give her. He would never love her—and sex was simply a poor substitute. A very pleasurable substitute, it was true—but she knew that it would eat away at her if she allowed it to continue. And surely it would destroy her when it stopped... 'No,' she lied. 'I don't.'

He smiled. And maybe that would be best for all concerned, in view of what had just happened. 'Well, I have a proposition to put to you which I think will satisfy both of us,' he said slowly.

Angie knew Riccardo well enough to sense danger. 'Prop-proposition?' she questioned.

'You know that I'm travelling out to Tuscany for my sister's wedding?'

'Of course.'

His black eyes glittered. 'Well, I want you to come with me.'

Confused, Angie stared at him. 'You're kidding?'

Riccardo allowed himself a slow smile. If she left his employment it would be a bore and an inconvenience—and he was intolerant of anything which spoiled the smooth running of his life. But he could cope with disruption. What he could most emphatically *not* cope with was the fact that his little Miss Mouse had been driving him crazy with desire and he couldn't get her out of his mind. Like some invisible and persistent itch, she had burrowed beneath his skin. So that he'd found himself waking in the night—hot and hard as he imagined losing himself in that deceptively sweet body of hers.

Clearly, such a situation could not be allowed to continue—and once he lost his desire for her, then the working situation *would* become intolerable. And

Riccardo knew there was only one sure way to lose an appetite—and that was to feed it! So he would have her. Take her. Glory in her beautiful body as many times as he wanted her. Then she could walk away—and they could both get on with their lives.

'No,' he said grimly. 'I'm not kidding. I want you to come to Tuscany with me.'

CHAPTER EIGHT

SHE did not want to go. *She did not want to go.* The words spun round and round in Angie's head like a mantra. But words, no matter how fervently they were felt, didn't change a thing. Not when you were up against the might and determination of Riccardo Castellari.

Angrily, Angie finished laying down the last neatly folded silk shirt and then slammed shut her suitcase, glancing down at her watch and realising with a fast-beating heart that Marco would be here with the car at any moment to take her to the airport. Her palms felt clammy and she felt slightly sick.

It was bribery.

Blackmail!

How *dared* Riccardo insist that she accompany him to Tuscany for his sister's wedding? she had demanded to know, in that flushed and uncomfortable period after their passionate bout of office sex.

'You will join me, ostensibly as my *secretary*,' he had

drawled. 'But we both know that you'll be fulfilling another role quite perfectly. As my *mistress*.'

'But, Riccardo—'

'No, say nothing more—for I will not countenance your objections. It is the perfect solution,' he had mused. 'My mother would not tolerate me bringing a lover into the house—but nobody need ever know that you are fulfilling a duel role so effectively, *cara mia*. You can provide me with sweet delight to distract me from all the stultifying details of the forthcoming wedding.'

'But why, Riccardo?' she had breathed. 'I mean, why *me*?'

Almost impartially, he'd studied her and it was then that Angie had realised how cold a colour black could be—for his eyes had looked positively icy as they flicked over her distressed face.

'Because you have unlocked a certain, inexplicable *hunger* in me, *cara mia*—and I see no reason not to feed that hunger until we are both satisfied. You have already decided to leave my employment, so lets make sure that when you do it is with no lasting regrets on either side.'

He had made it sound so *impersonal*—as if he were dealing with *something* rather than *someone*. Like a man who had just conducted an audacious boardroom coup. Defiance had reared its head. 'And if I object?'

Arrogantly, he had pulled her towards him—brushing his lips over hers in an almost negligent kiss, which had soon had her shivering beneath it.

'You won't object,' he had boasted softly. 'You want me far too much to dare to object.'

She had tried. Oh, she had tried. Overriding her hungry body's screaming protests, Angie had shaken her head and whispered *no*. And that was when clever Riccardo had played his trump card. If she agreed to the trip, he would let her leave his employment as soon as they returned to England.

'But I don't have a job to go to!' she had objected.

'What if I give you six months' full salary—and we'll call it a bonus for all your hard work?'

For a moment Angie had hesitated—some instinct making her feel uneasy about the deal. Was such an agreement wrong? And yet, wouldn't she at least be able to preserve her sanity this way and didn't she *deserve* some kind of bonus for all the hours she'd put in for him over the years? In the end, she had shrugged her shoulders and agreed and he had kissed her again, taunting her—telling her that her body could not deny how much she wanted him.

Picking up her suitcase, Angie stared in the mirror at her pale face and the set of her lips. It was true. She *did* want him—but her desire wasn't straightforward, like his. Hers was complicated by feelings—intense feelings for him which wouldn't seem to die, no matter how high-handed and hateful he could be. And surely she needed to work on herself—to try to cure herself of an unrequited love which could never have a happy ending.

In the end, it was that thought which convinced her

to agree with Riccardo's outrageous plan. She only knew the man she saw most days in the office—in his guise as highly successful businessman. She'd never seen him wearing anything other than a suit—or nothing at all. But surely if she was with him for a whole week—then she would see him for what he really was. An arrogant man with many flaws who was undeserving of her love.

She prayed that would be the case—because the alternative was terrifying. And what she couldn't bear would be the thought that she might become one of those sad women who carried a torch for someone who didn't care. The kind of woman who wasted her life, pining for someone who never even gave them another thought.

Her doorbell rang. Angie gave one last, nervous flick of her hair. That would be Marco. Riccardo had flown out to Tuscany yesterday afternoon—so at least she would be spared travelling with him. But she still had Marco to face. She hadn't seen Riccardo's driver since he had dropped his boss off after the Christmas party, when he must have sat outside her apartment for ages before deciding that his boss was there for the night. And she *liked* the driver—she didn't want him thinking of her as some kind of loose woman.

'How long does the journey take, Marco?' she asked him, once her suitcase had been installed in the capacious boot and they were speeding towards the airport.

'Should be there in just under the hour, *signorina*— the roads are quite clear,' replied the Italian, his equable tone temporarily setting Angie's mind at rest. It didn't *sound* as if he was judging her, she thought cautiously.

Angie had never travelled first class before—in fact, her whole flying experience had been a couple of package holidays to Spain. But in the event, it was wasted on her. She poked uninterestedly at the delicious slices of rare roast beef which the stewardess carved for her; she even failed to be tempted by the chocolate mousse. Her stomach was too tied up in knots to face eating—though she did drink a glass of champagne which, for a while at least, gave her a little courage at the thought of facing Riccardo again.

But her nerve nearly failed her when she walked through and saw him standing at the far end of the arrivals hall, waiting for her. A Riccardo who wasn't wearing his habitual, perfectly tailored suit. A much more casual and relaxed Riccardo and one she wasn't quite sure she recognised.

As she approached her eyes couldn't help drinking him in—even though she kept trying to tell herself that he was a cruel man to have insisted on her presence here as his mistress. After years of loyal service couldn't he have just let her go with some dignity—and let her quietly fade into the background?

But his dazzling appearance eclipsed the troubled nature of her thoughts. He was wearing jeans—black jeans which clung to every lean sinew, emphasising the powerful thrust of his thighs and reminding her of things she would much rather forget. A dark sweater and soft leather jacket completed the buccaneer image—his black hair was ruffled and the olive skin glowed with life and health. But despite the outwardly relaxed appearance, nothing could disguise the hungry gleam which sparked his black eyes as she grew closer.

His gaze raked over her with predatory insolence and just for a moment Angie allowed herself to marvel at the fact that he really *did* seem to desire her very much indeed. *He*, Riccardo Castellari—billionaire tycoon—desired *her*—his plain little secretary. Hadn't he told her that himself—even if he had tempered the words by shaking his dark hair in disbelief, as if such a thing was incredible.

But it *was* incredible, wasn't it? Here she was, ordinary Angie Patterson—walking across the shiny floor of the arrivals lounge towards the man who was dominating the attention of just about every other person in the place. Shouldn't she just try to enjoy it?

Lie back and enjoy it? mocked the voice of her conscience.

I've got nothing to be ashamed of, she told herself fiercely. I'm a single woman and he's a single man and we're hurting no one. Straightening her shoulders, she lifted her chin and walked up to him in her new high-heeled boots.

'Hello, Angie,' he murmured, and gave her a slow, lazy smile.

Angie's heart leapt—until she told herself to read nothing special into the fact that his black eyes had momentarily softened. Of course they had. What man's wouldn't have felt a moment of fleeting affection for a woman when she'd had her legs wrapped round his back on the floor of his office yesterday? And that was the sole reason she was here today—so he could repeat the erotic exercise as often as possible. But that didn't mean Riccardo had suddenly acquired a deeper, more significant way of looking at her. That was all in her head.

'Hello, Riccardo,' she said, her voice coolly polite.

He observed her demeanour with a mocking smile. 'So you have brought a little of the English frost with you, is that it?'

'What did you expect—that I'd be leaping for joy having been blackmailed out here?'

'Don't be melodramatic, *piccola*—you could have easily stayed at home.'

'And turn down the chance of a pay-off and early exit from your life?' she challenged hotly.

'Why, Angie,' he murmured. 'And here was me thinking that you were here because you couldn't resist my body.'

Glaring at him, she glanced around. 'Shh! Somebody might hear!'

He shrugged as he took the suitcase from her unprotesting fingers. 'We're speaking English,' he remonstrated silkily. 'And we're in Italy—where men and women tend to be less uptight about such matters.'

'Oh, how you twist things round to suit yourself!' she retorted crossly. 'One minute you're advocating harsh rules that virgin women should marry older men—and the next minute you're telling me that Italy is liberal about lovers.'

'Ah, but that's the difference between lovers and prospective marriage partners,' he murmured flippantly.

Reinforcing her lowly status, the careless remark hurt more than it should have done and Angie dropped her passport into her handbag and zipped it up, determined to change the subject. 'What did your sister say when she knew I was coming?'

'She's delighted—if a little distracted—but I guess that's the prerogative of brides-to-be. Shall we go?'

Angie had half expected to see another chauffeur-driven car—since that was usually Riccardo's preferred mode of transport—hoping that a third person might dilute some of the undeniable tension between the two of them. But her wish was not to be granted since an airport valet brought round a sleek, scarlet statement of a car which she realised that Riccardo was planning on driving himself. She swallowed. Just her and him. Alone together in a confined space, while her nerve endings were screaming out their heated response to his proximity.

Her pulse skittered as he pulled away from the kerb and the powerful car began heading out towards a line of mountains. Determinedly, she stared out of the window— afraid that he might read some of the conflict of emotions in her face. Or worse, the naked desire in her eyes.

Yet despite her misgivings, she soon began to relax a little—lulled by the sheer beauty of the green countryside which flashed past and by the smooth progress of the car.

'It's amazing,' she said softly.

'My driving, you mean?'

'No.' She laughed, in spite of her nerves. 'The countryside. The country itself.'

'But of course. It is the most beautiful country in the world,' he said. 'We have sleek cities and ancient villages. Stunning beaches and rich agriculture. Look up there and see the pure white marble which streaks the mountains like virgin snow, Angie. That is the same marble which Michelangelo used to fashion his David—which is the greatest sculpture in the world.'

She heard the pride and fervour which had deepened his voice—a side of Riccardo she'd never seen before, and one which was oddly stirring. Had she been naïve in hoping that prolonged exposure to this man might remove her longings for him? What if the reverse were true—her passion for him growing while Riccardo grew bored with her?

Surely here was a lesson to be learned. That she must protect her emotions at all costs. She felt the car swing off the main road and then turned to him as they bumped their way up a lonely little track and came to a halt. 'This isn't where you live,' she said slowly as she heard the engine die.

'No.'

The confusion in her voice was genuine. 'Then what are we doing in the middle of—?'

'This.' He pulled her into his arms and stared down at her—a fierce dark blaze in his eyes. 'What I've been wanting to do since I first saw you walk towards me at the airport with that misleading butter-wouldn't-melt look on your face. To kiss you, Angie.'

It occurred to her that he could have kissed her back then—but maybe that would have been too public a display of affection for a secret mistress. People he knew might have been watching them and started asking questions; demanding answers. She was here as his secretary and the sex would be furtive—as if he were somehow *ashamed* of what he was doing.

'I—'

'Shh.'

His lips silenced her and all her objections were banished in that first sweet touch. She heard the low growl of appreciation he made and for a moment she luxuriated in the pleasure of being in Riccardo's arms again. Of being able to tangle her fingers in the rich silk of his ebony hair and for his raw, musky scent to invade her nostrils like a welcome marauder. Desire flashed over her skin like sheet lightning.

'Riccardo,' she breathed.

'Angie,' he murmured back, briefly removing his lips from the soft petals of hers to stare down at her. 'You've been driving me crazy with wanting, you know. It's insane but I just can't stop thinking about yesterday. About how we…how we…' His fingertip seemed to be activated by memory as he began to trail it down over her cashmere coat. All the way down the thick barrier until he reached the hem, which sat primly over her knees.

She held her breath as the finger tiptoed underneath before he began sliding his hand slowly up over her thigh. Let him, she thought greedily. Let him touch me just for a minute and then I'll stop him. She closed her eyes as the direction of his hand became more purposeful. Now it was skating even further upwards—tracing light erotic circles over each inner thigh and causing her to expel a breathless little gasp.

She could feel the stealthy and inexorable heat building. The responsive prickle of her breasts. The clamouring of sexual hunger which hadn't featured in her life for so long that she'd almost forgotten it—and yet which Riccardo had activated and which now burned with a fierce flame inside her.

'Riccardo!' She caught his face between her hands as his fingers skated over the hot and aching core of her—the barrier of panties and tights doing nothing to lessen the growing hunger within her. Her throat felt constricted, her cheeks on fire—and then she realised that he was now pulling at the belt of her coat.

He wanted her here—in his car—down some little Tuscan track! His furtive secretary lover.

Her body screaming its protest, Angie wrenched herself out of his arms. 'Stop it,' she whispered from between lips which felt swollen to twice their normal size. 'Stop it right now.'

A nerve worked at his temple. 'You don't want me to stop it.'

Maybe her body didn't—but her dignity demanded

it. Or did he think he was just going to erode that too with his sexual mastery—the way he had chipped away at her heart?

'Oh, yes, I do.' Ineffectually, she pushed at the hard wall of his chest. 'Do you really want me to turn up at your house and to meet your family with my cheeks all flushed and my hair awry—making it perfectly obvious what we've just been doing?'

'They won't care what you look like,' he snapped insultingly.

'I find that very hard to believe,' she returned, enjoying the outrage on his face as she dared to stand up to him. 'And even if they don't care—then I most certainly will. I'm here as your secretary, remember? And there's a certain standard to maintain—a decorum— which I don't intend to compromise with a quick fumble in your car!'

'A quick fumble?' he echoed, outraged.

'Well, what would you call it?'

'You do not think that such an experience would be pleasurable?'

'N-no.' She was on less sure ground now. 'I'm not saying that at all. You're very good, as I'm sure enough people have told you. I'm just refusing to turn up to your house giving people ammunition to make negative judgements about me.'

Struggling to rein in his ragged breath and trying to ease the unbearable ache at his groin, Riccardo glared at her. This was no coy little game she was playing, he realised with dawning disbelief. She really meant it. Did she think that he would fall under her spell if she resisted him?

And yet he could not remember the last time a woman had spurned his sexual advances.

For a moment, an unwilling respect warred with his feelings of frustration—and then he moved away from her with an impatient click of his tongue and started up the car.

'Riccardo—'

'Don't talk to me when I'm driving!' he thundered.

'But you've left the handbrake on.'

With a curse, he released it—wishing that his body could be freed from its tight, aching constriction with such ease. Then he forced himself to concentrate on a road which suddenly seemed unfamiliar—though he had driven along it many times since the age of seventeen. He would make her pay in his bed tonight, he thought angrily. And she would suffer such sweet torture for the frustration she had dared inflict on him.

In the simmering atmosphere of the car, they didn't exchange another word until they had descended a winding mountain road and they came to a small village. Angie looked out of the window, captivated by all she could see. There were lots of little houses and a clutch of shops, which were shuttered up for the afternoon, as well as a small schoolhouse, and a beautiful grey-stone church. And through it all snaked a river—crystal-clear and fast-moving as it curved a silver line through the green pastures.

Up one of the steep adjoining side-roads Riccardo drove, until at last he reached his hilltop destination and then he stopped to allow her that first view—the view which always took people's breath away, no matter how rich or how jaded their appetites.

'The Castellari home,' he said, with an unmistakable ring of pride to his voice. *'La Rocca.'*

Their stand-off forgotten, Angie stared at the family home which she'd heard him mention over the years. She had always known it was a castle—had even talked about it to her mother—but the reality of actually seeing for the first time took her breath away. It really *was* a castle!

The pale and ancient stone building rose up out of the stunning landscape, its castellated ancient walls and loophole windows overlooking gardens which were speared by the deep green arrows of cypress trees. Against a backdrop of mountains were orchards into whose trees had been hung beautiful lanterns—presumably to help light the bridal procession.

'Oh, it's beautiful,' she breathed, turning to look at him—her eyes shining with wonder. 'Absolutely the most beautiful place I've ever seen.'

And something in her genuine regard soothed his jangled nerves, made him nod his head in quiet agreement—acknowledging an enthusiasm which was sweet rather than avaricious . He had never brought a woman here before, he realised with a start—until he reminded himself why. Bringing a woman here was a big deal, which might have hinted at a permanence he did not intend. And not for a moment did he underestimate the powerful allure of this ancient place, which commanded all the land which surrounded it. It was a place which people—especially women—would covet, and that was why he kept them away.

But this situation which had arisen between him and Angie was different. He did not need to keep batting off hints that the relationship might become something more—or have to guard his tongue to ensure that nothing he said might give his lover the wrong idea. His relationship with his secretary was based on honesty and mutual desire—which was undistorted by false romanticism.

He drove in through wrought-iron gates and stopped in front of a huge wooden door. Inside, the entrance hall was vast, lined with aged wood and lit by a roaring fire. A sleeping cat briefly lifted its head, yawned—and then resumed its sleep.

'Come and meet my family,' he said as he slipped the coat from her shoulders and hung it up and then shrugged his way out of his own leather jacket. He glanced down at his watch. 'They'll probably just be finishing lunch.'

Angie followed him through a maze of corridors towards the sound of voices speaking in Italian—but not particularly congenial voices, she realised. A woman's was raised in obvious protest and a man was clearly arguing with her.

She followed Riccardo into a formal dining room—not really having time to take in the splendour of the huge space—because there was something else which was much more noticeable than all the wealth and history contained within these walls. Angie frowned. A man and a woman sat at opposite ends of the table— but there was absolutely no laughter or mirth on their faces. They might as well have been at the reading of a will, judging from their expressions.

Their dark colouring and naturally sensual features immediately marked them out as brother and sister and she could see something of Riccardo in both of them. But more than anything else, Angie was drawn to the pale, pinched face of the bride-to-be and the haunted look in her eyes.

And the instinctive thought flashed through her mind that this didn't look like a woman about to participate in one of the happiest days of her life. This looked like a woman who was fast-tracking her way towards doom.

CHAPTER NINE

'You remember my sister, don't you, Angie?' questioned Riccardo as he led her into the room.

Angie nodded—hoping that her bright smile hid her shock at seeing Riccardo's young sister again. Why, she looked positively *gaunt*—her high cheekbones like two high shadowed slashes arrowing down to her nose. Surely that amount of weight loss was due to something more than just pre-wedding nerves?

'I certainly do. Hello, Floriana, nice to see you again— and congratulations on your forthcoming marriage.'

A faint frown criss-crossed the girl's lovely face as she summoned up an answering smile. 'Hello, Angie,' she said. 'It's nice to see you again, too. We are…we are pleased to have you here. My mother sends her apologies for not being here to greet you herself. She's dealing with caterers at the moment and she looks forward to seeing you at dinner. So does my bridesmaid—she's English, too.'

'Aren't you forgetting to mention someone, Floriana?'

drawled a silken voice from the opposite end of the table. 'I'm sure that Riccardo's guest is looking forward to meeting the *Duca*.'

Angie turned towards the dark-featured man who was reclining with indolent ease in one of the chairs, still wearing riding clothes.

'But I don't believe you've met my brother, Romano?' murmured Riccardo.

Angie shook her head. She'd certainly remember if she had. So this was Romano Castellari—another stalwart of the international gossip columns, as single, sexy Italian billionaires tended to be. In a way, the brothers looked remarkably alike—with their jet hair and imposing physiques. But this man's features were, if anything, even harder than those of Riccardo and there was a coldly formidable air about him. She knew that he was the elder of the two and that he ran the vast Tuscan estates owned by the family. 'No,' she said, slightly nervously. 'But I've heard lots about you.'

Romano gave a detached kind of smile as he rose with effortless grace to shake Angie's hand, his black eyes flicking over her with cynical interest.

'All good, no doubt?'

'Oh, I couldn't possibly say—everything Riccardo says to me is in the strictest of confidence,' answered Angie gamely, hoping to lighten the inexplicably dark mood which pervaded the room, but Floriana's sombre look remained firmly in place.

'It's very good of you to bring your *secretary*,' commented Romano, raising his black brows in arrogant question. 'I do hope you aren't planning on working *all* the while you're here, Rico?'

'I have a couple of important deals going through,' murmured Riccardo. 'And I decided that Angie deserved a little treat since she's threatening to leave me.'

'Really? What a pity—you must be sure to change her mind. Good secretaries are so hard to find. By the way, we've put her in the west wing—which, as you know, is at the opposite end of the house from where you're sleeping. I do hope that won't inconvenience you too much if you have to…*work* late.' Romano's black eyes flashed a mocking challenge at his brother and Angie suddenly went cold inside. He *knows*, she thought. He knows that the two of us are lovers—and he *doesn't approve*.

'You'll meet my bridesmaid later,' said Floriana. 'She and a whole group of others are staying at a hotel in the village. Romano thinks it would be too distracting to have a lot of people here—though heaven only knows, there's enough room.'

Angie felt a sudden flick of envy as her tongue flicked out to moisten her lips. Oh, to be staying in the village—far away from this cold house with its strange atmosphere and its complicated menfolk. 'Perhaps I could go and unpack now?'

'Sure,' said Riccardo. 'I'll show you the way.'

'Have fun,' murmured Romano. 'I expect we'll see you at dinner. Don't work *too* hard.'

Angie didn't say a word all the way back through the seemingly endless journey to her room, where her case had magically appeared—presumably placed there by some unseen servant. Uncaring of the huge bed or the magnificent picture-postcard view which could be seen from her window, she turned angrily on Riccardo.

'Your brother *knows*!' she accused.

'Knows what?'

'That…that…that we're *lovers*!'

'Are we?' he murmured as he pulled her into his arms and pushed the hair away from her face. 'You've kept me waiting for so long that I'd almost forgotten.'

Half-heartedly, she tried to pull away from his embrace but her body seemed to have other ideas. 'He *knows*,' she repeated.

'He doesn't know. He's guessing—and so what, Angie?' Tipping her chin up, he raked his gaze over her. 'Are you ashamed?'

Was she? She was angry with herself for being here, yes—for allowing herself docilely to be led, like a lamb to the slaughter. And for accepting so little from him, when she wanted so much. But ashamed? She shook her head as she looked up into the soft, dark gleam of his eyes, feeling her heart begin to pound and the over-whelming urge to have him touch her. 'No, I'm not ashamed,' she whispered.

'Then kiss me.'

'No.'

'Kiss me, Angie. If, as you say, my brother has

guessed—then why should we endure all the innuendo without any of the pleasure?'

His arguments were beating down her objections and his lips were making resistance impossible—trailing fire where they touched. Her head fell back as they whispered along the curve of her jaw, the long line of her neck, and she shivered as he reached around her back. Unzipping her dress in one single, fluid movement, he eased her arms out of the garment with the skill of a man who had performed this particular task many times, until it pooled in a soft heap by her ankles.

'*Piccola,*' he murmured, unbearably turned on by the sight of her in that so plain underwear she wore. Despite the short notice, by agreeing to accompany him here—any other woman would have moved heaven and earth to acquire the flimsy wisps of underwear which would be expected of the mistress to a wealthy man. But she had not. And although he knew that her failing to do so was more in a spirit of defiance than anything else, there was still something ridiculously *innocent* about her functional bra and briefs, this miserable pair of tights. His lips drifted along the line of her collarbone. 'You look…'

Not used to be being stripped naked in the middle of the day, Angie froze defensively. 'What?'

'Beautiful,' he murmured, realising to his surprise that he meant it.

Something in his voice stirred her just as much as the practised fingers which were reacquainting themselves with all her secret places—touching her softly and with unerring precision. Her senses began to sing, her blood heating her skin as he set her body alight. So why not just enjoy this? Take all the pleasure he was offering and stop wanting the impossible? To be his equal in the bedroom even if she was his subordinate outside it. Sliding her hands beneath his sweater, she began to run her fingers hungrily over the oiled silk of his back.

'So are you,' she whispered back.

Her urgency transferred itself to him and Riccardo momentarily moved her away while he peeled off his jeans and sweater, giving her one brief, provocative smile before tumbling them both down onto the bed. Their limbs tangled warmly as her lips sought his. Her arms wrapped him tightly to her, pulling him closer with an eagerness which made him give a low laugh of pleasure. For a moment their eyes met in a silent look as he straddled her, then drove into her with that first, longed-for thrust, which made her cry out until he kissed her quiet.

And Angie began to tremble. It felt as if she had entered another dimension of living. As if this melding together of flesh was what nature had intended her for. Even her orgasm seemed to happen in slow motion— almost miraculously at the same time as his. She heard the helpless cry he made, so that afterwards she found herself lying dazed in his arms, completely shaken by what had just happened. And for a while they just lay there, and that closeness was almost as good as what had preceded it.

'Oh,' she murmured eventually.

Absently, he stroked her tousled hair. 'Good?'

'A-amazing. Well, you know it was.'

He found himself asking a question he never asked women. 'And how do I compare with your other lovers?'

She found the query intrusive, and yet wasn't there a part of her which wanted him to know that she *didn't* behave like this with other men? 'I think you know that you're a marvellous lover,' she said quietly. 'As for comparisons, I think they're odious, but if you must know— I've had one lover before you, and it was a pretty disastrous experience.'

Riccardo felt the surface of his skin suddenly growing cold. How come she always told you more than you needed to know? So that the answer to a simple question suddenly seemed to carry a whole weight of significance. Wasn't it easier to think of her as someone who'd been around a bit—rather than as someone who had briefly had her fingers burnt by a man? 'What a pity,' he murmured non-committally.

Angie turned onto her side to study the hard, perfect profile of his face. 'There seemed to be a lot of…tension going on downstairs.'

He shrugged. 'My sister is getting married the day after tomorrow. What do you expect?'

She hesitated. 'There's a difference between nerves and tension, Riccardo—and she seemed to have been having some sort of argument with your brother.'

'That's because she has insisted on having a woman

as bridesmaid whom Romano thinks entirely unsuitable for the task.'

'But surely it's her decision, not his? Nothing to do with him?'

'It's certainly nothing to do with *you*,' he returned softly. Rubbing a thumb over the rasp of his chin, he yawned. 'I'd better go.'

But Angie couldn't help noticing the exhaustion in his face; the dark shadows beneath his eyes—and, despite his prickly attitude, she felt her heart soften. Caring about Riccardo's welfare was an impossible habit to break, it seemed. Gently, she began to stroke his black hair until she saw him relax and saw his eyelids shuttering—as if he were fighting the temptation to close them. Why not let him sleep—just for a little while? 'Close your eyes,' she whispered. 'Just for a minute.'

Pulling the duvet over them both, she snuggled herself against his body, hearing his sigh and echoing it with one of her own as she heard his breathing steady into sleep.

Much later, she woke—feeling hungry and realising that they'd eaten no lunch—and she was just thinking about waking Riccardo when she felt him stir next to her.

For a moment he felt as if he was in the most comfortable place on the planet. His knee was thrust between two soft thighs and he could hear the even sounds of a woman's breath as it fanned against his shoulder. For a moment he sank into the feeling, revelling in the sensations which were whispering over his skin before he realised where he was—and then he swore softly in Italian.

'Che ora e?' he snapped, lifting his wrist to glance at his watch. He sat up, his face wreathed in anger. 'Why the hell did you let me sleep?'

Dismayed, Angie stared at him. 'Because you looked as if you needed to.'

Jumping out of bed, he grabbed his jeans and began to pull them on. *'Madre di Dio!'* he exclaimed furiously. 'You've certainly changed your tune! From worrying about what my brother might think of our behaviour—you switch to luring me into staying.'

'I didn't *lure* you!'

'You covered me up with a duvet,' he accused.

'Is that such a heinous crime?'

It felt like a trap. A trap as seductive as those great big eyes of hers and her warm, soft body. He shook his head. 'I don't want to spend half the afternoon in your bedroom!' he declared.

'Then don't! Nobody's keeping you here. Go!'

'Oh, I'm going all right.' He pulled the dark sweater over his naked torso and turned his back on her while he zipped up his jeans—wanting to distract himself from the alluring sway of her naked breasts and the still rosy flush which darkened them. And only when he had mentally doused himself with the equivalent of a cold shower did he feel able to turn and face her again with his customary cool.

'Right—you'd better know what's happening,' he

clipped out. 'There's a formal dinner tonight here in the castle—you'll need to wear something smart. And did you bring your laptop with you?'

His statement had started her mind start buzzing—wondering what to wear to the formal dinner—but the subsequent question threw her in her tracks. 'Er, no. I didn't think I had to.'

'Really?' he questioned coolly. 'Well, in that case I'll have one sent up here. I want you to chase up the Devonshire account for me. There are plenty of scenic locations around the estate where you can work.' He walked over to the door, seeing the outraged expression on her face, and he paused. 'What's the matter, Angie—surely you *were* expecting to work? That, after all, is the reason you're here. The sex is simply a perk.'

It was possibly the most hateful thing he could have said and presumably he meant it to be—but Angie didn't react. She would not give him the pleasure of knowing how much his words could rip right through her. When would she ever learn that their agendas were completely different? 'Of course,' she answered, as if nothing would bring her greater pleasure. 'And I might as well tidy up the Posara portfolio while I'm at it.'

His eyes narrowed. 'If you must.'

And, oh, wasn't it worth the act of pretending that his words hadn't hurt—just to see that rare look of uncertainty which had crossed his arrogant face? 'Close the door behind you, would you?' she murmured. 'I want to take a shower.'

But after he had left, she did not head for the bathroom—she didn't think her shaky legs would carry her. Instead she sat down on the rumpled mess they'd made of the bed and wondered what she was *doing* here. Had she thought it would be easy?

Yes, in a way—perhaps she had. Which only went to prove how short-sighted she could be. She had always associated arrogance with Riccardo—but hadn't she been guilty of an arrogance of her own? Thinking that she could handle her emotions both in and out of his arms. But she couldn't. Women weren't built like that—or, rather, she wasn't.

When he was making love to her it was all too easy to imagine that it was for real. That her years of quiet devotion had finally borne fruit and that they were a proper couple. But it wasn't real, and they weren't. It was just amazing sex—something he happened to be extremely good at. And if she was being honest—wasn't it likely that *every* woman he took to his bed felt the way she did? As if she wanted him to sweep her into his arms and tell her that he loved her and couldn't bear to live without her.

Well, it wasn't going to happen—not in a million years. And deep down she *knew* all this—so when was she actually going to start believing it? Nothing was going to change unless she made it change—so maybe she needed to start being a bit tougher in order to protect herself.

For the first time, she allowed her eyes to drift around

the room and to acknowledge how truly beautiful it was. Rich brocade drapes shimmered like precious liquid metal at the windows and similarly rich fabrics were used in the heap of cushions piled onto a sofa. There was a writing desk, too—antique and lovingly polished and very beautiful.

Angie unpacked her case and then headed off for the bathroom—which was as gleamingly modern as the castle itself was old. Rich soaps and shampoos were lined up and she washed away all traces of the journey and Riccardo's love-making—before emerging pink and scented. Wrapping herself in a giant towelling robe, she walked back into the bedroom to see that a laptop had been placed on the desk in her absence, and she stopped in her tracks.

He certainly hadn't wasted any time in driving home her real status! Flinging a load of mundane tasks at her even though they'd only just arrived. Angie picked up a brush and began to pull it through her wet hair. Well, the work could wait. She was through with being useful, doormat Angie. Angie who took just whatever Riccardo Castellari cared to chuck at her. Because she was slowly beginning to realise that Riccardo treated her the way he did *because she let him*!

And she wasn't going to let him. Not any more.

The thought empowered her and, seeing that there were almost two hours until the formal dinner, Angie spent ages drying her hair, then settled down with a book. It was a very good book and she felt especially pleased that she had been able to push Riccardo out of her mind enough to really get into the story.

In fact, she was two thirds into it when she saw that there was only half an hour to go before dinner. Hastily, she put on some make-up and then opened the wardrobe—wondering if she had the courage to wear the only dress which would be suitable for a grand event in a place like this.

It gleamed provocatively at the back of the wardrobe—the red dress which she had been unable to resist bringing and which she had vowed she would never wear again. But it was strange how seductive a beautiful garment could be. And Angie wasn't stupid—she recognised that it had a power all of its own. Beside it, her own conservative clothes looked boring and so *safe*—no matter how much she tarted them up with accessories. How could she *not* wear it?

Her hands were trembling as she slipped it on, because of course this was much more than a dress—it was imbued with significance. Riccardo had bought it for her. It was what she had been wearing the night he had taken her to bed. It was what had made him stop looking *through* her—and realise that she was a woman.

Was it too risqué an outfit in which to meet his mother? she wondered as she slowly circled in front of the mirror. No. The designer was world famous and Italian women were famously stylish. And Riccardo's mother won't *care* what I wear, she thought. To her—I am just someone he employs. She'll barely notice me.

There was a knock at the door and Angie's heart raced. Would Riccardo approve? Would he perhaps try to kiss her—to mollify her after his earlier display of anger? Well, this time she wouldn't let him.

But it was not Riccardo who stood at the door. A young female stood there, looking rather diffident—her plain dark dress marking her out clearly as a servant.

Just like me, thought Angie with a pang—only I expect that this young girl doesn't get any of the 'perks' which Riccardo pointed out earlier. *'Buona sera,'* she said hesitantly. *'Como si nama?'*

The girl's English was as hesitant as Angie's Italian, but her smile was wide. 'My name is Marietta. You…you follow me?'

'Of course. Thank you.' But it was strange how feelings could suddenly switch. From dreading seeing Riccardo, Angie could now feel herself fervently wishing that he'd come to collect her himself as all her bravado slipped away. How could she walk into a room full of important people she didn't know—all proper invited guests, apart from her—with even some members of the aristocracy thrown in? Would they look at her and judge her, and find her wanting?

She heard the murmur of voices and the chink of glasses as she descended the curving wooden staircase. Taking a deep breath, she told herself that she looked fine but inside she was trembling like a leaf. Pinning a smile to her shiny lips, she began to walk down towards the assembled guests—a rainbow display of finery contrasting with the dark suits worn by the men. A dazzling and glamorous assembly. Some of them looked up and some turned around.

But all she could see was the ebony spotlight of Riccardo's eyes following her every movement.

CHAPTER TEN

'WELL, well, well—I see that you have decided to dress
like the siren for the party tonight, *piccola*.'

Riccardo's words were silken-soft but the look which
accompanied them was anything but. The coal-dark
glitter of his eyes moved provocatively over her face, the
quick flick of his tongue over his lips reminding Angie
of how they'd just spent the afternoon. Bringing back
with aching clarity the slow, almost drugging quality of
their love-making.

Angie shook her head, trying to clear her head of the
memory. 'But you bought me this dress, Riccardo,' she
protested, taking a proffered glass of *Prosecco* from the
passing waitress. 'And surely the whole point was to
wear it?' She glanced around at the other women, reassured to see that some were in gowns which made hers
look positively demure. 'Unless you're saying that it's
unsuitable for the occasion.'

There was a pause. The only thing about it which was
unsuitable was the fact that it reminded him just what lay

beneath it. A nerve flickered at his temple. 'You know very well that it's suitable. In fact, you look more beautiful than any other woman in the room,' he countered.

'You don't mean that.'

'*Sì, cara,*' he said steadily. 'I do. Now, you'd better come and meet my mother.'

'I'd love to.' But her cheeks pinkened at the unexpected compliment as she looked around. 'Where's the bride-to-be?'

With narrowed eyes, Riccardo checked out the room, his tone doing nothing to disguise his disapproval. 'She still hasn't shown.'

'Oh, well—it's the bride's prerogative to be late.'

'That's not supposed to be until the wedding day,' he returned acidly. 'There's still two days to go.'

'And what about the groom?'

'The *Duca* is standing over by the woman wearing diamonds.'

'Every woman is wearing diamonds.'

He laughed. 'He's by the fireplace, but don't stare, Angie—it's rude.'

Angie didn't need to stare—one quick glance was enough to surprise her so much that she stared down into the fizzing bubbles in her drink in an attempt to compose herself. Surely Floriana couldn't be marrying *him*! She took a sip of the wine. The *Duca* was elegant, yes—but he must have been almost fifty, judging from the harsh lines on his face. And wasn't that the hint of baldness at the crown of his head? He looked *ancient* in comparison to the beautiful young Italian girl.

She lifted her eyes to find a sudden coldness in Riccardo's—as if daring her to make the obvious comment. But why should she? As he had reminded her earlier—it was none of her business. 'Floriana's a lucky girl,' she said dutifully.

'Yes,' he agreed tersely. 'She is. Now come and meet my mother.'

Angie was aware of eyes following them as they made their way across the crowded room—before stopping in front of the matriarch of the family.

'*Mamma*, I told you that I was bringing Angie with me? And I believe you have spoken on the phone many times.'

Despite her elegant high heels, Riccardo's mother was surprisingly small and terrifyingly elegant. Her figure was as neat as a young girl's and she was clad in very obvious couture—a gleaming burgundy gown of heavy silk with a string of large, lustrous pearls around her neck. The two women shook hands and her black eyes looked Angie up and down with interest.

'So we meet at last,' she said, in perfect English. 'The woman who makes my son's life run like clock-work, or so he tells me.'

Angie blinked, slightly taken aback to hear *another* compliment and glad that Riccardo had gone over to talk to his brother—even though the two men were standing dominating the room, like a pair of dark and formidable statues. 'It isn't easy,' she joked.

'No, I can imagine,' came the dry rejoinder and then Signora Castellari smiled as she looked her up and down. 'And you look wonderful. I had no idea that your taste in clothes was quite so exquisite, my dear.'

There was an awkward pause as Angie tried not to flinch. What did she *say*? That it was a Christmas present from her son? Wouldn't that seem like much too intimate a gift from boss to secretary, and might it not make his mother raise her eyebrows—possibly in disapproval?

'Thank you,' she said weakly.

'At least I know that Riccardo must be compensating you adequately, if you can afford to dress that well.'

Angie nodded and raised her drink to lips which suddenly felt like stone as the elegant woman moved away to greet another guest, hoping that her face didn't betray the terrible sense of distress that her innocent remark had provoked. Because Signora Castellari had said nothing untoward; not really. She thought that she was simply meeting her son's long-time secretary—she wasn't to realise that the secretary in question was also his lover, which made innocent remarks about financial compensation acutely embarrassing.

At that moment, there was a stir of expectation from the guests and everyone looked up towards a second staircase to see Floriana slowly descending the staircase with a girl by her side whose pale skin and unruly red curls marked her out from the mainly Mediterranean gathering. That must be the bridesmaid, thought Angie.

Floriana's black dress was stark and her own hair was piled up into an elaborate creation on top of her head, fixed with small diamond pins. Round her neck were more diamonds—a veritable waterfall of glittering icy stones. She looked, Angie realised with a shock, like a mannequin. As if she were composed of wax instead of flesh and blood.

But then they were being called into dinner and, to Angie's relief, Riccardo came to accompany her to the table. 'Surely you can't seat this many people all at once?' she whispered.

'Wait and see.'

The dining room—well, it was more of a hall—was absolutely beautiful, lit by hundreds of tall candles and scented rather overpoweringly with lilies. A single long table was draped in snowy linen and glittered with gold and crystal. Angie found herself seated next to a very sweet old man who had once spent a holiday in Brighton and who was eager to practise his English. On her other side was a teenage cousin of the groom who was clearly bored out of his mind and would rather have been somewhere else.

At the opposite end of the table and next to Riccardo's mother she could see the *Duca* holding forth, with a morose-looking Floriana by his side. And on opposite sides sat the grim-faced Romano and the red-haired bridesmaid who seemed to spend the majority of the meal glaring at one another. What was *their* problem? Angie wondered as she lifted her napkin, thinking that this made *her* little sister's pre-wedding party look like a match made in heaven.

Although delicious, the meal seemed to go on for ever, and if Angie was full up after the pasta course no one seemed to notice or to care whether she ate or not. She told herself she was glad Riccardo was sitting far away from her. Yet her feelings were at war with common sense—she ached for his touch, no matter how much she tried to tell herself that she was a stupid fool for wanting him.

Did she make those feelings apparent? Was that why when she looked up from her unwanted plate of sorbet to find herself caught in the crossfire of his gaze his black eyes seemed to mock her while his lips curved into a smile of sensual promise. Angie swallowed. He was so…so *sure* of himself, wasn't he? So certain of her—that no matter what he said or did, she would still sink into his embrace whenever he snapped his fingers.

And you will, won't you? Because despite all your little pep talks about no longer being a doormat, aren't you secretly counting off the seconds until you can feel him in your arms again?

After dinner, there was dancing in a huge ballroom which had been decked out with garlands of scented blooms and shiny balloons in silver and gold. It seemed that every VIP and dignitary from miles around was attending and Angie told herself that of *course* Riccardo wouldn't ask her to dance—and that even if he asked she would refuse. She would sweetly tell him to go and entertain his guests and not his employee. But she was wrong—on both counts. He *did* ask, and she didn't refuse—because when it came to it, how could she? Not when her heart was racing with excitement and her skin tingling when he laid his hand on her bare arm.

'Having a good time?' he murmured as he pulled her against him, splaying his fingers over the buttery satin of her dress.

It wasn't her role to spoil his fun and to tell him that she thought this was the strangest atmosphere she'd ever encountered at a pre-wedding party. And besides, those thoughts were fading from her mind already—eclipsed by the sheer pleasure of being in his arms again.

As they danced, sensations began to bombard her—wearing down a resistance which was already thin. She was aware of his own particular musky scent and the now familiar feel of his hard body against hers. Angie certainly wasn't an accomplished dancer, but she didn't need to be because Riccardo was guiding her around the dance-floor with a sure touch which made her feel positively graceful.

'Mmm?' he prompted, his lips close to her ears.

'I'm…I'm having a great time,' she answered truthfully, because in that moment she couldn't think of a place she'd rather be.

'Me, too.' Tightening his hands around her waist, he looked down into her flushed face. Saw the way that her lips had parted. Noted the tiny pulse which hammered at the base of her throat. And suddenly he wanted to kiss her. Damn the ballroom, he thought. And damn the guests with their quick and curious eyes. Riccardo swallowed, pulling her even closer—wanting to demonstrate just how aroused she had made him. 'I may just take you out for the day tomorrow,' he added. 'If you're lucky.'

Angie's heart missed a beat. *If you're lucky.*

Maybe the words weren't intended to be patronizing, but that was how they came across—or maybe it was because they were accompanied by the shameless thrust of his pelvis, so that she could feel the hard heat at the very cradle of him. It was nothing but a silent and arrogant sexual boast and it seemed to mock at her own romantic interpretation of the dance, making her feel stupid. Angie pulled back, ignoring the screaming objection of her body. 'Sorry, but I'm afraid I'll have to work tomorrow.'

He stared at her blankly. 'Work?'

'That's what you supplied the laptop for, remember?'

He was in such a state of frustrated desire that she might as well have been speaking in Greek for all the sense he made of her words until his head cleared. 'But you did that work this afternoon,' he said quickly.

'No, I didn't.'

'You didn't?'

Angie allowed herself a serene smile. 'No. I took a long bath and read a book instead, actually.'

A pulse began to flicker at his temple. Was this the beginning of rebellion—of Angie abusing her position simply because they'd become lovers? Why, in all the years of working for him she had never refused to carry out one of his orders. 'That's not what I wanted,' he snapped.

'Well, it's what *I* wanted,' she returned.

'But I'm paying you to do what *I* want,' he reminded her with silken cruelty.

'No, you pay me to support you in a secretarial role.' The words came out in a breathless rush, fuelled by a fury at what he'd just said and suddenly Angie didn't care that they were in the middle of the dance-floor. Because wasn't this long overdue? 'Don't you think I've done enough out-of-hours for you over the years to recognise when I deserve some time off, Riccardo? If you trust me enough to make me privy to all your confidential business dealings—then you should credit me with the judgement to decide when I want to ease off!'

There was a stunned kind of silence for a moment, and then he smiled. 'Oh, *cara*,' he murmured. 'Your insubordination is such a turn-on that I can hardly wait until I get you into bed again. If only I'd realised that I had such a little wildcat hiding away all these years.'

'Well, you're the one who's made me into a wildcat,' she returned, without thinking.

'Am I really? Then at least I have something to be grateful for.' Trickling his thumb down over her hips in what felt like a proprietorial marking of his territory, he bent his mouth to her ear. 'But you will forgive me if I leave you now. Much more of this on the dance-floor and I shall be dragging you off to the nearest alcove to peel off your panties and that really wouldn't do, would it?'

And without another word, he turned and walked away and Angie was left staring after him with flaming cheeks and a hammering heart. Had he meant to drive home that her impact on him was purely physical? She felt faint, dizzy, and wondered how soon she could decently slip away from here—away from the eyes which she sensed were looking at her with open curiosity.

Distractedly, she went to the side of the ballroom and was just thinking about making her escape when she felt a tap on her shoulder and she turned to see Floriana standing there.

Up close, her mannequin-like appearance was even more apparent and Angie thought that the girl's lips looked positively bloodless. Pushing thoughts of Riccardo out of her mind, Angie forced a smile. 'Lovely party,' she said.

'Thank you.' But Floriana's smile didn't meet her eyes. 'Angie, would you like to come and see my wedding dress?'

'Me?' questioned Angie in surprise.

'*Please*. You'd like to, wouldn't you? I thought that all women liked wedding dresses.'

Telling herself she should feel flattered, Angie nodded. 'Of course, I'd love to.'

'Then come with me—but let's be quick,' the Italian girl urged. 'Before Romano accuses me of neglecting my guests.' Linking their arms as if they'd been lifelong friends, Floriana led her along one of the long corridors alongside the ballroom and which led to yet another staircase. At the top of the stairs was Floriana's bedroom and as she pushed open the door Angie could see the gleam of ivory satin beneath Chantilly lace.

'Oh, it's beautiful,' she exclaimed, walking over to where the gown hung, marvelling at the delicate fabric and thinking that this was the kind of wedding dress that little girls sometimes dreamed of. 'Absolutely beautiful.'

'Isn't it?' said Floriana, but her voice was flat as she shut the door and Angie turned round, her eyes narrowing with concern.

'Floriana, is…is something wrong?'

There was a pause as the girl raked long olive fingers through her fringe, dislodging a diamond pin in the process but ignoring it as the precious clip clattered to the floor. And eventually, like someone who had finally thrown in the towel, she nodded. 'I can't marry Aldo,' she breathed. 'I just can't do it!'

Realising that the girl was trembling, Angie walked over to her and put her arm round her shoulders, thinking how bony and birdlike they felt. 'Listen— every bride gets nerves,' she soothed, realising that she was echoing what Riccardo had told her. And you didn't believe him, did you? 'It's perfectly natural.'

'No!' Distractedly, Floriana moved away. 'It isn't that, believe me. People keep telling me it's nerves, but it's not. I've allowed myself to get into a situation which should never have happened. I feel as if I've sleepwalked my way into a nightmare. Angie, *I can't go through with it*!'

Angie stared at her uncomprehendingly. 'But why are you telling *me* all this?'

Dark brown eyes were fixed on her unwaveringly. 'Because you are an outsider.'

Angie flinched.

'And you must be a sensible woman to have been employed by Riccardo for all these years. You will not tell me what you think I should hear. You will tell me what I must do.'

'That's too big a responsibility,' Angie protested, shaking her head.

'Please.'

'What about your brothers?' questioned Angie. 'Can't you confide your fears in them?'

'In *them*? You have to be joking. They are so keen for this marriage that I suspect they would march me down the aisle!' said Floriana bitterly. 'They are nothing but tyrants!'

There was a long pause while Angie considered what to say. But Angie knew she couldn't look into the frightened eyes of a woman panicking on almost the eve of her wedding, and pretend that everything would be all right in the morning.

'And does Aldo—the *Duca*—does he know how you feel?'

'I've tried speaking to him but he will not listen,' whispered Floriana. 'His mind is set on this wedding. He would never allow it to be cancelled. Every time I say something it is as if I have not spoken at all. For I am his trophy bride—his innocent virgin—or so he thinks.'

Angie's eyes narrowed with comprehension as she

realised what Floriana had just told and its possible implications for the future. Was purity an essential factor in this marriage? Remembering what Riccardo had said about his own desire to marry a virgin, she supposed it was.

'Are you afraid to go through with the wedding because you think that your sexual experience will disappoint your husband—is that it, Floriana? Because I'm sure if you explained—'

'No.' Floriana's stark word interrupted her. 'That is not the reason why. The reason is much more simple that that, Angie—you see…' She shrugged her shoulders helplessly. 'I simply do not love him—not the way a woman should love the man she is about to marry.'

For a moment Angie said nothing—because what *could* she say? And yet—did the words come as a great surprise to her? No, of course not. You would need to be blind not to have noticed the lack of chemistry between the engaged couple. Gently, she placed her hand on the girl's arm. 'Then you must have the courage to tell him that,' she whispered. 'You *must.*'

Leaving Floriana sitting on the bed, Angie somehow managed to find her way back to her own bedroom without having to return to the party. Stripping off the red gown, she washed off all her make-up before climbing into bed, bone-tired now, the comfort of the soft bed soothing her troubled senses as she lay there worrying about the outcome of Floriana's revelation.

Should she tell Riccardo? As she lay there in the darkness Floriana's disconcerting words came flooding back to her. *'They are so keen for this marriage that I suspect they would march me down the aisle!'*

Would he really go that far? Somehow she doubted it. But would Romano?

Her mind buzzed uncomfortably but the long and emotional day had worn her out and she must have dozed off, because when she awoke it was to the sensation of a warm, naked male getting into bed beside her and then a mouth edging luxuriously over her breast.

'Riccardo?' she murmured sleepily.

'Why, were you expecting someone else?'

'I…*oh*!'

'Oh, what, *piccola*?'

'I must…' Struggling against the blissful sensation of his tongue trailing a warm, sensual path over her bare skin, Angie's hands moved up to his shoulders. 'Riccardo—I must talk to you.'

'Not now.'

'But—'

'I said, not now,' he growled. 'I have been wanting to do this all night.'

She told herself that there was no point in bringing up a contentious subject when it was past midnight and nothing could possibly be done. That she would tell him in the morning—in the cold clear light of day. But wasn't some of her reasoning bound up in the fact that he was now kissing her, and she couldn't prevent herself from sinking into that kiss? So that he became the central focus of her world and in that moment nothing outside it existed?

Dreamily, Angie tangled her fingers in his hair and kissed him back as he began to make slow, sweet love to her—the feel of his body deep inside hers washing away everything except pleasure itself. Afterwards their lips stayed touching—locked in a lazy kind of kiss—and with a jolt Riccardo remembered back to earlier, when they were dancing. Thinking just how much he wanted to kiss her. *Kiss* her? In the darkness, his eyes snapped open. This was getting dangerous. Crazy.

Beside him, Angie stirred, murmuring her way into sleep, but Riccardo's eyes stayed open—he knew that he must leave the warm comfort of her bed before he was tempted into staying all night. And it wasn't just the thought of the servants' gossip, but his own reluctance to wake up beside her which made him wait until he was certain she was asleep. Then he pushed aside the covers and dressed in the inhospitable darkness.

It was icy-cold as he made his way to his own room, where he slept fitfully, waking to the sound of loud banging, which he thought was all part of the strange, Angie-fuelled dream he'd been having—and it took him a moment to realise that someone was at *his* door and it was morning.

'*What the hell is going on?*' he raged.

Romano appeared in the doorway, still buttoning up his jeans, his face a study in anger as he shot out a few terse Italian sentences at his brother, and minutes later Riccardo was dressed and storming through the castle towards Angie's room.

She was clearly fresh out of the shower—wrapped in a towel with her hair all wet—and sitting by the window reading a book with that innocent look which belied her bedroom antics. He felt the heavy twist of lust and anger.

'Riccardo!' she exclaimed when she saw the look of dark fury on his features. 'Is something the matter?'

'You tell me,' he snapped. 'Exactly what do you know about my sister's disappearance?'

'Her *disappearance*?' The book slid from her fingers and Angie stood up, her heart pounding so loudly she felt as if it would deafen her. 'Why, what's happened?'

'That,' Riccardo said grimly, 'is what I intend to find out. My brother tells me that you and Floriana were seen leaving the party last night. What the hell did she say to you?'

Angie swallowed. She *should* have told him last night. She should have done. 'That she couldn't bear to go through with the wedding. And that...that she didn't love Aldo.'

'So she confided in you?'

'Yes, I suppose she did.'

'Why you—a stranger?'

She stared at him. How much of the truth could he take? she wondered. 'Maybe because she felt that nobody else would listen,' she whispered.

His face remained cold and obdurate. 'So what did you say?'

The question whipped out like the accusation it was clearly intended to be and Angie realised that Riccardo was not interested in home-truths. It was facts he wanted and facts he could deal with, not emotions. Ignoring the look of disdain which iced from his eyes, she forced herself to concentrate, telling herself that she would not let him intimidate her.

'I told her that it was better she speak to Aldo. To sort it all out with him. Has she done that?'

'Has she done that?' He gave a bitter kind of laugh. 'No, Angie, she has not done that. What she has done is to have left a note which currently has my mother in hysterics and the castle in chaos. And she's taken her damned passport and is on her way to England with that dumb bridesmaid of hers unless Romano and I can stop them!'

Angie's fingers flew to her lips. 'Oh, my God!'

'Didn't you realise that my sister has a history of this kind of behaviour? That there was a man in her past— some *Englishman* she thought she was in love with when she was at school. Who has now reappeared on the scene and made my crazy sister believe that she still loves him?'

'N-no. I…of course I didn't.' Angie met the fury in his black eyes. 'But that shouldn't make any difference, Riccardo. It's still *her* life. She's old enough to make her own mistakes—if that's what it is—and it isn't necessarily a mistake just because *you* don't happen to agree with it! You can't force her to behave how you want her to behave!'

'Didn't you think—?' He took a step forward and saw her bite her lip, but he was so angry that he couldn't think straight. 'Didn't you think that it might have been an idea to speak to me about it?'

'I *was* going to tell you—'

'But just not last night, hmm?'

'It was late. You were tired.'

'And you, *cara*, just couldn't wait to get me to…'

He said something in Italian which Angie didn't understand, but she didn't need to be a linguist to comprehend its crude meaning.

'All you were thinking about was your own damned pleasure!' he finished witheringly, and saw her flinch.

'Actually, I *was* going to tell you—only you slipped from my bed in the night, like a thief!' she retorted. 'But now when I stop to think about it—what good could you have done, Riccardo? Because when a girl like Floriana is in some kind of turmoil, why try to involve someone like you—who has the emotional capacity of a gnat?'

His fists clenched. 'How dare you speak to me in this manner?' he hissed.

'And don't you dare pull rank on me at a time like this!' she stormed back. 'Either Floriana is old enough to be married, or she isn't. And if she is—then she has to learn to stand on her own two feet and not take advice from her two brothers who are treating her like some kind of puppet simply because they like to control the world and the people in it!'

Riccardo's nostrils flared in aristocratic disdain. 'That is *enough*,' he grated. 'You know nothing of these matters, Angie—you are a member of my staff who is here as my guest.'

'Not any more, I'm not. I resign as of now!'

His black eyes were cold. 'You'd better get your stuff packed and I'll have someone drive you to the airport. The place is in chaos and there's no point in you staying.'

Angie swallowed down the great lump which had lodged itself in her throat. 'I'll have my desk cleared by the time you get back to London.'

At this, he stilled—and pushed his face a little closer to hers, noting with some masochistic kind of satisfaction that her eyes automatically darkened. 'Spare me the melodrama, *cara*. You will clear your desk when I tell you to,' he bit out.

'But you said…' Her breathing coming in short, painful puffs of air, she stared at him. 'You said I could leave straight away with six months pay if I came out to Tuscany with you,' she whispered.

'Did I? Well, in view of your behaviour—I've changed my mind.' He gave a grim kind of smile. 'Such a verbal agreement between two lovers simply boils down to your word against mine. Next time I'd get something down in writing, if I were you.'

CHAPTER ELEVEN

ALL the way during her miserable flight home to London, Angie told herself that she didn't care. That Riccardo wouldn't dare blackmail her into staying under what would now be intolerable working conditions. That he didn't have a leg to stand on.

But it didn't work out like that.

She spoke to a lawyer—a friend-of-a-friend told her that her boss *was* completely within his rights. For one brief second Angie contemplated opening her mouth to ask whether the fact that they'd been lovers might have any bearing on the case, then quickly shut it again. Because that made her sound at best unprofessional, and at worst... Well, it made her sound completely lacking in morals. As if she were one of those awful women in the workplace who tried to further their career by less than scrupulous means.

But she was worried about Floriana, too—and now wondering whether she'd done the wrong thing. If she'd told Riccardo late that night, then could her disappearance have been prevented?

She was shivering as she caught the Tube into work, full of a cold which seemed to have hit her the moment she'd landed back in England. And full of dread too, because yesterday she had received a matter-of-fact email from Riccardo telling her that he was back from Italy and would be returning to the office this morning, prior to flying out to New York at the end of the week.

Angie bit her lip. With a bit of luck, he might be abroad most of the time she was working out her notice—and with a bit more luck, she might find a decent job to go to in the interim. She'd actually managed to arrange a couple of interviews for the following week.

She was banking on him strolling in at around ten, but fate was clearly conspiring against her because he entered the building at exactly the same time as her and, bizarrely, they met in the middle of the vast marble foyer, staring at one another like two strangers.

'Hello, Angie,' he said, in a cool kind of voice.

The last time she'd seen him he had been yelling at her—so was the fact that this was a very public meeting place the reason why at least he *sounded* civil? She matched his tone with a cool, non-committal one of her own. 'Good—good morning.'

She was forced to share the lift with him and the presence of two women from the accounts department thankfully ruled out any attempt at conversation. But the silence pressed down on her like a lead weight and

Angie could feel tiny beads of sweat springing from her forehead as she tried to look somewhere—anywhere—other than at that hard and handsome face, which still had the power to make her heart melt.

Riccardo let his eyes drift over her. She was pale, he thought, and she looked as if she'd lost weight—was that possible in a matter of days? His mouth hardened. So she'd lost weight—why should he care? Hadn't her stubbornness helped complicate an already complicated family situation?

The lift doors slid open and he stood back to let her pass—aware of the faint, light scent she wore and the gleam of her hair as she moved. He followed her into the office, unable to keep his eyes from the sexy sway of her bottom—even though he had told himself countless times during the last few days that the affair was over, and that he would arrive back in London and wonder what the hell he'd ever seen in her.

So what had gone wrong?

Why did he find himself wanting to pull her into his arms again and seek comfort and passion in those soft, seeking lips of hers? He wasn't quite sure—and, for a man to whom uncertainty was a stranger, Riccardo felt oddly unnerved by the sensation.

After she'd hung her coat up and blown her nose for what seemed like the hundredth time, Angie looked at him. 'How's Floriana?'

There was a pause as he looked at her, seeing the concern in her eyes and the faint tremble of her lips.

'I should be angry with you,' he said slowly. 'For letting precious time elapse after she left the castle.'

Angie seized on the one positive word in his statement. '*Should* be?' she questioned.

He gave a ragged sigh. 'But I thought about what you'd said—about Floriana needing to make her own mistakes—and realised that Romano and I might have taken our roles as surrogate father just a little too far.'

'You've found her?' she demanded.

'Yes. She's in England.' His mouth quirked in an odd kind of smile. 'She is getting married after all.'

'*Married?* But…but…how?' Angie frowned at him in confusion. 'She told me she didn't love Aldo—and I believed her.'

'It isn't Aldo.'

'*What?*'

'She is planning on marrying the Englishman— Max—the one she was involved with all those years ago. It seemed that back then he did what he thought was the decent thing by ending it, having decided they were both too young. But it seemed that the very possibility of her marrying another man was enough to bring him to his knees and back into her life—and for Floriana to realise what it was she really wanted.'

Angie stared at him cautiously. 'And how have your family taken it?'

Riccardo shrugged. 'The reaction, as you can imagine—has been mixed.'

All he knew was that his sister was ecstatic, his

brother and Aldo were livid and his mother was—oddly—quietly contented. She had pointedly told him and Romano that love was the *only* reason why a couple should marry! Something which had startled Riccardo out of his complacency zone. And here he had been—all these years—labouring under the illusion that, just because his own father had been two decades older, his parents had simply worked hard at a marriage of convenience. It seemed that he had been very wrong indeed.

'I'm very pleased that it's all worked out so well for her,' said Angie.

'Are you?'

'Yes. No one should enter a marriage with that degree of dread,' she said quietly, and then started coughing.

Black eyes narrowed as they scanned her face and he noticed that her nose was red, in contrast to the almost translucent paleness of her skin. 'Are you okay?'

'I'm all right. I've just got a…a…ah-ah-*shoo*!'

He frowned. 'You shouldn't be at work.'

'It's only a cold.'

'You shouldn't be at work,' he repeated obdurately.

Her eyes met his in a mocking challenge. 'I thought that absenting myself from your office wasn't an option, Riccardo. I thought I was to work out every second of my notice or risk legal action. I thought—'

'Angie,' he cut into her words roughly. 'I said those things in anger and when I had time to think about them, I realised I shouldn't have done. In fact, I realised a lot of things, the main one being that I don't want you to leave.'

Wasn't it ironic how words you once would have taken to your heart and cherished could no longer have the power to thrill you when they were spoken too late? Life, thought Angie bitterly, was all a question of timing.

'I was unreasonable,' he continued, when still she didn't speak.

From somewhere Angie mustered up a smile. 'So no change there.'

'Can we forget it ever happened?'

She looked at him. For a highly intelligent man he could be so dense. Or maybe it was just that innate arrogance of his, which he sensed would always carry him through. He just didn't realise, did he? 'We can try,' she said gamely.

Riccardo slanted her a slow smile. 'So you'll stay, after all?'

There was a pause. Once she would have been unable to resist the power of that look. 'Riccardo, I can't do that.'

Suddenly, the smile left him. 'Why not?'

'Because I can't; not now. Not now we've been lovers—it can never get itself back onto the right kind of boss-secretary footing which we used to enjoy. And you'll find another secretary.'

He curled the fingers of his hand into a tight ball. 'I don't want another secretary.'

'But you will—and it will all be fine. You just don't like change, that's all.' And oddly enough, she felt strong now—despite the slight woolliness in her knees which seemed to go hand in hand with the brass band which was currently playing a muffled symphony inside her head. 'The row we had was irrelevant, I was planning to leave before we had it and I'd be planning to leave no matter what. I have to—surely you can see that?'

'But why?' he demanded.

Tell him, Angie urged herself. Explain the feelings and some of the emotions behind your actions and you won't be able to see him for dust. 'Because sooner or later our...*affair* will finish—and it would be intolerable to go on working together after that.'

Riccardo scowled, unused to having this kind of argument put to him, when he was the one usually calling the shots. 'It isn't an affair,' he objected stubbornly. 'Since neither of us are married.'

But she noticed he hadn't denied that it would finish. For how could he? 'Then how would you define it?'

He shrugged. 'A relationship?'

She heard the doubt in his voice and she might have laughed if it didn't hurt so much. 'A working relationship, yes—but nothing more than that. Why, we've never even been out on a date together!'

'Are you saying that's what you want?' he demanded. 'To start dating?'

She shook her head in frustration. 'Not at all,' she answered.

'No? Can't think of anything else you might want?' he questioned silkily as he pulled her to her feet and into his arms, his lips moving over hers with a hunger he made no attempt to disguise. Through the mists which now seemed to be gathering force inside her head, Angie felt the answering tug of desire, but she pulled away from him while she still had the strength.

'You'll catch my cold,' she objected and then, inexplicably, her teeth started chattering.

Frowning, he put the back of his hand over her forehead. 'You're burning up! That is no cold,' he ground out. 'That feels more like fever.' Exclaiming softly in Italian, he sat her back down on the sofa and quickly clicked out a number on his phone before beginning to speak in rapid Italian. '*Sì, sì—subito.*' And then he picked up Angie's coat and bag. 'Come on, *piccola*,' he said softly. 'We're going.'

Blankly, she stared up at him. 'Where?'

'I'm taking you home. You need to be in bed.'

'I don't—'

'Please don't argue with me, Angie. Not this time.'

She allowed him to take her downstairs, vaguely aware of curious faces turned in their direction once they reached the reception area. And dimly, once she'd been clipped into the seat belt in the back of the limousine, it occurred to her that Marco was taking a very odd route to Stanhope.

And it wasn't until they had pulled up outside a very impressive old building and a doorman had sprung into action—doffing his cap at Riccardo and pressing the lift button—that Angie realised that he wasn't taking her home at all. At least, not to *her* home.

'What are you doing?' she sniffed weakly as he held

onto her elbow and the lift zoomed with the speed of a jet towards its lofty destination. 'I thought you were taking me home.'

'You think I'd leave you there, in that tiny, miserable little place? All alone,' he added. 'With nobody to look after you?'

'I don't need anybody to look after me,' she said stubbornly.

'Yes, you do.'

She gave up objecting then because Riccardo carried her—*carried her!*—into what was clearly the master bedroom and her head felt all whoozy as he put her down on a huge bed.

Then he undressed her with a detached, almost ruthless efficiency—leaving her wearing just her bra and panties and pulling a sheet over her while he went to phone the doctor.

'I don't need a doctor,' protested Angie, even though she was shivering quite badly now.

The doctor arrived shortly afterwards and put a horrible cold stethoscope against her chest while he took her temperature. 'Her temperature is sky-high,' he announced.

She tried to grab the duvet, but Riccardo prised it from her fingers.

'You have a fever,' he reprimanded sternly.

'You must make sure that your girlfriend drinks plenty,' said the doctor. 'And takes regular analgesia. It's a nasty dose of flu which is doing the rounds, but she should be better in a few days.'

Angie wanted to protest that she wasn't his girlfriend, but now someone had started a steam train chugging inside her head. Weakly, she lifted her head from the pillow. 'I can't stay here for ah-ah-*shoo*…'

'Rest,' said the doctor severely.

'Oh, I'll make sure she rests,' said Riccardo grimly.

And in truth, it was bliss—almost worth being ill for. Because Angie had never been cosseted like this before. Even when she was younger, it was Sally, her younger sister, who was always fussed over. Sally who had undisputedly been Daddy's girl and so devastated by his death that she had demanded the focus of attention from their grieving mother. And Angie who had always helped provide comfort for both of them. Reliable Angie who just got on with things and never complained.

For two whole nights and two long days, she drifted in and out of a sweat-filled sleep. Once—very blurrily— to find Riccardo with his sleeves rolled up, sponging down her naked body with tepid water. Feeble hands fluttered up in a half-hearted attempt to cover her modesty, but he removed them from her burning breasts with a grim-looking expression on his face.

He wondered what she would say if she realised that last night she had deliriously been clinging to him and begging him not to leave her. And it had taken every bit of will power he possessed to cover her up with the thin cotton sheet instead of climbing in and taking her shivering body into his arms, as she had been demanding.

But on the third day, Angie awoke to the smell of

coffee and the sensation of someone having removed the cotton wool which had been padded inside her head. Blinking furiously, she looked around her in disbelief— her rapidly clearly mind taking in the colossal proportions of the bedroom she was in with something approaching disbelief.

She was in Riccardo's bedroom! Lying in his bed. Alone.

She looked around. All the furniture was very old and gleamed like silk and on the walls hung exquisite Tuscan landscapes. A vase of pure white roses drifted out a subtle scent and giant windows overlooked the verdant sweep of Green Park. Against her skin, she could feel the buttery caress of some soft material and, lifting up the sheet, she saw that she was wearing some sleek sort of nightgown—its eau-de-nil silk falling demurely to her ankles. Where had *that* come from?

Her legs felt so weak that getting out of bed took a little time, but after a few seconds she felt steady enough to move and made her way into the en-suite bathroom with the certainty of someone who had been there before, though not quite remembering when. Staring at herself in the mirror, she resigned herself for a shock— and a shock it certainly was.

Her hair was all over the place and her cheeks looked quite hollow—she must have lost at least five pounds. But the colour was beginning to return to her cheeks and her eyes looked surprisingly bright. Finding an unused toothbrush and some soap, she freshened up—using one of Riccardo's brushes to try to create some kind of order out of her ruffled hair.

Back in the bedroom she could hear the sound of a radio and activity in another part of the apartment and she went to find the source of it. And there—in a streamlined kitchen, looking remarkably proficient—was Riccardo busying himself with a coffee pot. He was in a pair of dark trousers and a silk shirt, his feet were bare and his black hair was not yet dry from the shower.

He must have heard her enter because he turned round and looked at her, his eyes running over her assessingly and, stupidly, Angie found herself blushing. It wasn't so much because she felt undressed—he'd seen her wearing a lot less than this. It was just that in a way this felt more intimate than anything which had gone before. *But it isn't,* she reminded herself fiercely. It's simply masquerading as intimacy.

'You're looking better,' he murmured approvingly. '*Much* better.'

'I feel much better. Riccardo—' She wrapped her hands around her arms. 'What's been happening?'

'You've been ill,' he said softly. 'That's all.'

'Then you've been…been…'

'Not now. Sit down. Please.' Waving aside her stumbled words, he pointed to a squashy black leather chair which was littered with cushions, and she sat down on it gratefully, her legs still weaker than she realised.

'Coffee?' he questioned.

She wondered if it occurred to him that their positions were suddenly reversed; that he was looking after *her*. Don't get used to it, she thought. 'Please.'

'And something to eat, I imagine? You must be hungry?'

'*Starving.*'

'Eggs okay?'

'Eggs would be perfect.'

He found himself humming as he melted butter in a pan and ten minutes later they were sitting side by side at his breakfast bar, eating scrambled eggs and raisin bread and drinking strong, dark coffee.

In between mouthfuls, Angie savoured the moment, even though she knew that it would be heartbreaking to relive it afterwards. They'd never done this kind of closeness before—though pretty much every other kind. And behind all the recent storms in their working relationship the bottom line was that they had always been a team. At least this way they would part on the good terms which their long partnership deserved.

'Thank you, Riccardo,' she said quietly. 'For looking after me so superbly.'

'I don't want your thanks.'

'Tough. You're getting them.' She saw him smile and she wanted to say to him: Stop smiling. *Stop being im possible not to love—and just start being impossible again!* But Angie knew she was fighting a losing battle—no matter how he behaved. For she had loved him when he had been impossible. Loved him in her bed. Loved him even through all the misunderstandings

and the angry words. She would always love Riccardo
Castellari, she realised—and that was the reason why
she needed to leave him. 'Anyway, after that delicious
breakfast—or was it lunch?—I guess I'd better be
getting out of your hair.'

Not only was it was a stupid expression, he reflected—but it was also completely inappropriate. He
couldn't think of anything he'd prefer right now than to
have her tangling those long fingers of hers in his hair.

His black eyes were fixed on her. 'Why not stay on
for a while?'

Her heart began to pound. 'Stay on?'

'Why not? There are more creature comforts here
than in your own place—plus staff downstairs who are
on tap to run errands for you. And I'm going to New
York later. Remember?'

Foolishly, she felt the sudden slowing of her heart
and a feeling of despair wash over her. Just how pathetic
could a woman be? What, did she think he was asking
her to move in because he'd been privileged enough to
nurse her through an unflattering bout of the flu?

'It's a very kind offer, but I couldn't possibly do
that,' she said.

'Sure you could, Angie. Enjoy a little luxury for a
change.'

She took a quick sip of coffee before he could notice
her wince. If he had meant to make her feel like Little
Orphan Annie, he couldn't have done a better job of it.
Could he picture her revelling in the non-clanking central

heating system and the thick, wall-to-wall carpets? And
did he pity her—going back to her tiny little apartment
and the almost hour-long journey to get there?

'I don't want to impose on your kindness any longer,'
she said stiffly.

Riccardo observed the proud and stubborn little set
of her lips, and sighed. She was still angry—as well she
might be—but surely a little time and a little rest might
have the power to dissolve some of those feelings?
'You're not imposing. I want you to stay here. Just enjoy
it—and let's talk when I get back.'

'Talk?'

He moved his face close to hers. Close enough for
her to feel the warm fan of his breath, but not quite close
enough to kiss. 'Let's just see how you feel about things
when I get back, hmm? Is that such an unreasonable
request to make, *piccola*?'

He knew so well how to be irresistible—damn him!
Because how could she refuse such an invitation when
it was what she really wanted? But if she stayed here—
supposedly to recuperate—then wasn't she in danger of
building castles in the air? Reading more into the situation than Riccardo ever intended her to?

Riccardo's eyes narrowed. 'You know that I'm not
going to take no for an answer,' he said softly.

'In that case, I guess the answer has to be yes.'

He smiled. 'Here are the keys. I've written down the
security code which gets you into the building. Now
enjoy,' he added.

'When will you be back?' she questioned.

'Not for a week. Stay as long as you like. And now, if you'll excuse me—I'll finish packing.'

This new courtesy was completely unexpected and Angie wasn't quite sure what motivated it, or whether she trusted it. And he hadn't made any attempt to kiss her, had he? After a while, he reappeared wearing a jacket to match the dark trousers and carrying a briefcase and small bag.

'Okay, I'm going. Get plenty of rest—understand?'

Angie nodded, and then he was gone.

Half hidden by one of the drapes, she stood at the window and watched him get into the dark limousine which was waiting outside the building and which was quickly swallowed up by the line of traffic heading west. And then the reality of what was happening suddenly hit her.

I'm staying in Riccardo's home. He told me to stay for as long as I liked. He's been looking after me while I'm ill and unless I'm still hallucinating—he seemed almost…tender this morning.

Did that mean anything? Would it be naïve to suppose it didn't—or foolish to suppose it did?

Probably a complete waste of time to suppose anything.

Instead, Angie began to make herself at home. The TV—which she eventually found hidden behind a sliding screen—was the size of a small cinema, and Riccardo had an extensive selection of films, including some amazing Italian ones which fortunately carried subtitles. Further investigation yielded a study which was crammed with books and had a sofa where you could curl up and read one of them.

When she felt better, she went out walking around Green Park and then mooching around the shops. Not that she bought anything—it just seemed such an incredible luxury to be within walking distance of all the West End stores. Riccardo rang her at lunchtime the following day—just as he was about to go into an early-morning meeting—and asked her if everything was okay and she told him that, yes, everything was fine. There was a sudden long pause in the conversation, as if he'd planned on saying something—but then he seemed to change his mind.

'And how's your sister—still getting divorced?' he asked, out of the blue.

Wryly, it occurred to Angie that they both had their share of troublesome sisters. 'I think so. I haven't heard much lately beyond the occasional frantic text and she never seems to look at her email.'

'Call her from my landline.'

'No, honestly—'

'Just call her, Angie,' he insisted.

She put the phone down feeling oddly warm—though this time her body heat had nothing to do with a flu virus. She'd never known Riccardo to be quite so thoughtful before—and when the phone rang later, she almost thought it might be him again.

'Hello?' she questioned softly.

'Hi.' It was a woman's voice—silky soft and with a twangy north-Atlantic drawl which tugged at a distant memory. 'Is this the maid?'

For a minute, Angie thought it might be a wind-up. 'No, this is…this is Riccardo Castellari's secretary.'

'Oh. Hi. This is Paula—Paula Prentice and I'm a friend of his.'

'How can I help you, Ms Prentice?' asked Angie, trying to ignore the terrified flutter of her heart.

'It's just that he has a red dress of mine—one I've never worn. It's a beautiful dress and Rico had it made specially and, well—it seems a kinda waste not to wear it.'

Suddenly, it all made sense. Of course. Riccardo hadn't broken the habit of a lifetime and bought her a present which might have required a little imagination or a little thought. Instead, she had been fobbed off with a dress which had been intended for another woman. A question of being in the right place at the right time. Or the wrong one.

It was one of those moments where, if she had been in a film, Angie might have dropped the phone and gasped. Or slammed the phone down. But although she might be a foolish, foolish woman who had read far too much into a careless gesture—she was the consummate secretary.

'Of course, Ms Prentice,' she said smoothly. 'Don't worry—I'll look into it and make sure it's all sorted out.'

'Thanks.'

After she'd put the phone down, Angie stared at it for a long minute, then lifted her eyes to look at the stars in the sky, remembering the night she'd been given the dress. Her innocent joy that Riccardo had bought her a gift which was intensely personal. A gift which had made her feel like a woman for the first time in her life. The dress which had transformed her enough to make Riccardo want to sleep with her. Had he been imagining that she was the other woman—the woman he'd *really* bought the dress for? Was that what he had thought of as he had thrust into her body with such passion that night—that she was really *someone else*?

Biting her lip, she looked around distractedly, as if suddenly recognising Riccardo's home for what it really was—alien terrain. Had she ever been stupid enough to think that she might have a legitimate place here? But she would not crumple. She just needed to keep busy. To keep *doing*. And she knew exactly what needed to be done.

CHAPTER TWELVE

WARM air ruffled through her hair and the sound of the ocean was as soothing as the head and neck massage she'd had earlier. Angie rubbed a little more sun-block onto her nose, and yawned. When it came to curing a broken heart—you couldn't get a much better location than an Australian beach, she decided as she lifted her face up towards the sun.

'Auntie Lina, Auntie Lina!'

A small dynamo of a child came bounding towards her, covering her with damp sand—and she giggled as her four-year-old nephew threw himself into her arms and clamped his cold arms around her neck. 'Hello, Todd,' she giggled. 'Did you have a good swim?'

'Mummy says I'm like a fish!'

'Then you must be *very* good! Angie glanced up to see her sister approaching, squeezing the water out of long hair bleached blonde by the sun. They hadn't been on a beach together since childhood—and how things had changed. When the two girls had been growing up it had been Sally who had been considered the pretty one—but since Angie had arrived, people had been commenting on how alike the two sisters were. And that had pleased Angie—not because of the implied attractiveness, but because it gave her a sense of belonging. A feeling of being part of something—a family.

She smiled at her sister. 'How was the swimming lesson?' she asked.

Sally grinned. 'Brilliant—though I'm exhausted. Thought I might go back to the house and get stuff ready for the BBQ tonight—do you want to come?'

Angie stretched out on the warm sand and shook her head. 'No. I think I'll stay here for a while—make the most of the sun while I can. Do you want me to look after Todd?'

Sally shook her head. 'No, he's tired. I'm hoping he might take a nap.' She hesitated as she picked up a towel. 'Listen, Angie…I don't know how to thank you.'

'I don't want thanks,' said Angie fiercely, because in truth she had welcomed the distraction of being concerned about someone else's worries for a change. She had gained a new perspective from her time with Riccardo, which had been useful when talking to her sister—and she had revelled in the opportunity of getting to know her gorgeous little nephew.

'Well, you deserve them,' said Sally. 'If you hadn't made me come to my senses. To realise just what I had—and that I was risking throwing it all away for nothing very much at all.'

Angie nodded. She had arrived at her sister's Sydney home with a heavy heart but a determination not to talk about the cause of it. Because Riccardo was firmly in the past and, besides, it was far too painful a subject to pursue. Not when her sense of betrayal felt so raw and her self-esteem had taken such a battering.

Instead, she had concentrated on trying to see whether her sister's marriage was really as doomed as she'd previously implied. She remembered the terrible atmosphere just before Floriana's planned wedding and that had given her an idea. Because there was never any doubt about how besotted Sally and Brad had been about each other on the day they'd wed.

'Try to remember just how much in love you were with Brad on the day you married him,' she had suggested softly to Sally. 'And take it from there.'

And, astonishingly, this simple tactic seemed to have set a reconciliation in motion. It seemed that Sally's husband Brad been working too hard—so he felt hard done by, while Sally felt neglected. A gulf had formed between them, which time had only widened. And yet, deep down, they had always loved one another. Angie realised that maybe just having a third person— someone who cared—pointing out the obvious could be enough to make people look at their situation in a different way. And Sally had so many blessings in her life—she'd just got out of the habit of counting them.

In the meantime, Angie had got to know her little nephew—which had given Sally and Brad the space for some quality time alone together. And it seemed that their love had blossomed again.

'And what about *you*?' Sally had questioned eagerly one night, over a large glass of wine. 'You're looking so good these days, Lina—it *must* be a man.'

Well, it was—and it wasn't. It *had* been a man. A man who had played with her—but who would never echo her love for him, despite their undeniable physical compatibility. But Angie had decided that she wasn't going to prolong the agony by confiding in her sister. The sooner she let it fade from her mind, then the sooner she would get over it.

So she told her sister that it hadn't been anyone special—and that was what she was still trying to convince herself.

She was just pulling a T-shirt over Todd's damp curls when she heard Sally make a small whistling sound.

'Oh, my—I think the gods have dropped a man straight from the heavens and he's walking our way!'

'You're a married woman,' teased Angie.

'I'm allowed to look. And he is *something else*. And he's…Lina, he's heading our way!'

What instinct was it that made Angie quickly turn her head to see the man her sister was talking about? With a disbelieving lurch of her heart, she recognised him immediately. The jet-dark ruffle of his hair. The lean musculature of his tall body. Although there were plenty of beautiful people of Italian origin in Sydney—Riccardo Castellari was in a league of his own.

'Who's that man?' demanded Todd, when he failed to get the attention of his mother or his auntie.

'Yes,' said Sally, turning slowly to her sister. 'Who *is* that man?'

Angie couldn't speak—the words she wanted to speak feeling like stones which were constricting her throat. What was he doing here? Why had he come to create more havoc in a life which she was trying very hard to live without him?

'He's my boss,' she said slowly.

Sally gave her a funny look. 'Your boss looks like *that*? Your boss who just *happens* to be walking along a beach towards you looking as if he'd like to shake you, or to…to…'

'To what, Mummy?'

'Nothing, darling,' said Sally hastily. 'Well, here he comes—and judging from the expression on his face, you'd better light the touchpaper and stand well back!'

Angie's heart was thundering beneath the silky little triangles which comprised the emerald bikini which she'd bought in one of Sydney's many beachside boutiques. She had known that inevitably she would run into him again—just not here and not now. Not when she hadn't planned her defences or practised the cool and uncaring face she was going to present to him when that day finally arrived.

The glitter from his black eyes was not particularly friendly. He stopped in front of her, and for a moment—just looked at her. 'Hello, Angie.'

Angie swallowed. 'Hello, Riccardo.'

They stood facing one another.

'Isn't anyone going to introduce me?' squeaked Sally. 'I'm Sally, Angelina's sister.'

'My name is Riccardo Castellari and I'm very happy to meet you, Sally—but I need a private word with your sister, if you don't mind.'

'Sure. Sure.' Sally started nodding persistently. 'Come back to the house later. Come on, Todd.'

Todd was staring upwards. 'Who's that man, Mummy?'

'He's a friend of Auntie Lina's. Come on—you'll see him later. Or at least, I *think* you will.'

Angie watched her sister and nephew walk back up the beach and her mouth dried. Because even though the white sandy beach was peppered with other bathers it felt as if the world had telescoped into that moment, leaving the two of them alone together, staring at each other like combatants.

What right did *he* have to look so angry?

'What are you doing here, Riccardo?' she questioned coolly.

Her insouciance made him want to haul her into his arms and crush her unreasonable lips beneath his. 'What do you think I'm doing here?' he demanded hotly. 'And why the hell did you do the big, melodramatic exit—leaving the damned country without a word about where you were going?'

What an arrogant nerve he had. 'Why do you think?

Because *Paula* rang—you remember Paula, the stunning Californian actress you dated for nearly a year—asking could she please have her red dress back. *Her* dress! The dress I stupidly thought was mine because *you gave it to me for Christmas*!'

His black brows knitted together. 'Is that what this is about, Angie—a damned dress?'

'Yes!' She shook her head. 'No!'

'Let me tell you about the dress.'

She wanted to put her hands over her ears. 'I don't care about the dress!'

'Well, I do—so you'd better damned well listen!' He took a deep breath. 'Paula ordered it from some fancy designer and put it on my account—without bothering to tell me. She used to do that kind of thing a lot. She wanted marriage, I didn't—so we split. Some time later—much later, as it happens—the dress was delivered to *my* hotel in New York. I didn't particularly want to renew any kind of communication with Paula and so I just brought it back to England with me. I was planning to give it to charity, to be auctioned off. And then something that day made me give it to you, instead.'

She knew exactly what that 'something' was. Deciding that her general frumpiness could do with a bit of a facelift, he had given the dress to his hapless secretary—without ever realising the knock-on effect if would have. Helplessly, Angie shook her head, trying to dispel the telltale prickle of tears which would make her dissolve like a fool in front of him. 'It doesn't matter how I got it, or why you gave it to me—although if you'd been honest about it from the start, it might have helped.'

'What, give a woman a dress and tell her that it was really meant for someone else?' he drawled. 'Even I know enough about the psychological processes of the female to know that's a non-starter.'

'You, of course, have had plenty of research opportunities into the psychology of the female!' she snapped.

Black eyes blazed into her. 'Maybe I have—but not one of them has been as stubborn and as infuriating as you're being right now, Angie Patterson.'

Tiredly, she shook her head—knowing that she'd read far too much into the dress; she could see that now. She couldn't keep blaming Riccardo. A casual gift from boss to secretary and she had reacted to it with the excitement of a woman who had just been presented with a large diamond ring. 'Anyway, it doesn't matter,' she whispered. 'The dress is just a symptom of the whole malaise. It made me realise how stupid I'd been. I should be grateful to the dress, really.'

Riccardo frowned. Now she sounded as delirious as she had been when she'd had the fever. When he'd seen her so helpless and vulnerable and he had bathed her body and fed her little sips of water, as tenderly as if she'd been a tiny kitten. 'What the hell are you talking about?'

She would never make him understand unless she told him, no matter how painful that was. 'The dress made me into…into someone I'm not,' she stumbled. 'Someone who could hold my own in your world. But

I'm not from your world, Riccardo, and I can't ever be. We should never have made the jump from colleagues to lovers. We just shouldn't.'

'You know you don't mean that, Angie.'

'Oh, but I do. Really, I do.' Yet wasn't that the hardest thing in the world to say—especially when he was standing there in jeans and T-shirt, his handsome face looking stubborn and unyielding? The man she had loved for so long that doing so seemed as natural to her as the sun rising in the sky each morning. Her heart full of heaviness, she realised that she hadn't asked the most fundamental question of all. 'Anyway, why are you here—and how did you find out where I was?'

'I asked your mother,' came the grim rejoinder as he held up his hand to halt this particular line of questioning. 'And I'm here because I want you back.'

Pain sliced through her and tears began to hover at the periphery of her vision. 'But I can't come back,' she whispered. 'No matter what you say. I can't work for you any more, Riccardo—don't you see?'

Impatiently, he shook his head. 'I don't want you to *work* for me.'

Angie stared at him in confusion. 'You don't?'

'No way—I've already given your job to Alicia.'

'To Alicia?'

'*Sì.* She's very good—you told me that some time back. Promising material for a secretarial post—and, of course, she doesn't answer back the way you do.' But then, no woman ever had. And no woman had ever communicated with him on such a fundamental level as Angie had. On every level, really. His rich voice hadn't once faltered, but now—for the first time in his life—it did as he met the wary shimmer in her eyes. And discovered for the first time in his life that something wasn't necessarily his for the taking, simply because he wanted it.

Once, he could have snapped his fingers and Angie would have come running—but she had changed, he realized, just as he had. She had put in place barriers to protect herself—which he must now tear down with his bare hands. And yet didn't her fierce pride and her dignity only reinforce his desire for her?

'I want you to come back to be with me, *cara mia*— as my partner, not my secretary. *Mia donna*. Because sometimes you have to have something taken away from you to realise just how much it means to you. Only it took me a little while to realise why every day seems grey—and maybe a little longer to realise what had been staring me in the face for so long.'

Love. Something he had schooled himself not to believe in—bound up in his own supposedly fail-safe recipe for a marriage. But events had demonstrated that his ideas were illusory. And his heart had made him as helpless as the next man. When he had come back from America and found Angie gone a pain incomparable to any other had ripped through him.

Catching her hand, he brought it to his lips while his black eyes blazed the intensity of their message. 'I say to you now words I have never spoken to another woman, *piccola*,' he said softly. 'And that is, I love you with all my heart.'

Heart hammering with fear and disbelief, she shook her head, not wanting to believe him…not daring to believe him. Fearful of the pain coming her way if he didn't mean it. 'No, you don't love me. You don't believe in love, remember? There's no such thing. It's "chemistry" and it's "lust".'

He flinched as she quoted his words back to him. 'I was a fool,' he admitted. 'An arrogant fool. But sometimes you have to experience something yourself in order to believe in it. And I love you, Angie,' he repeated softly.

Angie could do nothing to prevent the sudden, hard pounding of her heart. He was arrogant, yes—but his arrogance could be a loveable trait as well as a dangerous one. She thought about the woman she had been when he'd said those words to her. Back then she had been so desperate for his love that she had been completely desolated by his statement. She had been so lacking in self-esteem that she would have fallen on any crumb of affection he had carelessly tossed at her. But she was not that woman any more—and, really, it didn't matter what you owned or where you came from. True equality was when you gave and received love on a level playing field.

'Shall I tell you why I love you? Would you like me to?' he continued inexorably. 'Where shall I begin? Because you're beautiful—inside and out. Kind and sweet and strong and sexy. Because you are not afraid to tell me what you think. And because I never realised that someone who had become a friend could become such an exquisite lover.' He stared down at her, realising almost for the first time that she was standing there, wearing nothing except a flimsy little emerald bikini—and he had been so intent on getting his message across that he'd barely noticed her beautiful body. And that was a first, too.

'Do you believe me when I tell you that, Angie? That you have become as much a part of my life as the beat of my heart itself?'

The poetry of his words thrilled her and terrified her. Tremulously, she lifted moist eyes to his—scarcely able to believe what lay within her grasp, but knowing above all else that Riccardo always spoke the truth. 'Tell me again,' she whispered.

'I love you.'

'And again.'

He smiled. 'I love you.'

And as the last of the bitter barriers came tumbling down, she put her arms around his neck, her face close to his. 'I love you, too, Riccardo,' she whispered. 'So very much.'

Now he laughed, and anyone who knew Riccardo Castellari solely in the boardroom would have been taken aback by the carefree quality of that laugh. Tenderly, he pushed away a strand of hair from one damp cheek. 'Then why, *mia cara*—why are you crying?'

She stared up into his beloved face and her heart turned over. 'Because I'm so happy!'

And there, on a sun-drenched Australian beach—oblivious to the surfers and the swimmers—Riccardo pulled Angie into his arms and kissed away her tears, reflecting that feminine logic was indeed a very strange thing.

EPILOGUE

'Do you want to go down yet?' Angie gave her hat one final adjustment and then walked to the window to stare down at the beautiful gardens of the castle grounds. 'We've got plenty of time, but it's always better to be early for an occasion as important as this. And I'd like to have a look at the flowers in the church first.'

Riccardo gave a lazy smile as he let his gaze drift over his wife. 'In a minute. Just let me look at you first.' She wore a dress of deep violet which contrasted perfectly with her colouring—the pale skin and the big, green-gold eyes. Perched on her head was a feathery little nonsense of a creation in a matching shade. She looked, he thought, chic, jaunty and very, very beautiful.

Caught in the slow ebony scrutiny of his eyes, Angie blushed with pleasure as she read the expression on his face. For a man who had once declared himself a sceptic about love, he had been making up for it ever since, she thought. Big time.

They had married almost immediately after returning from Australia. Riccardo had wanted it, insisted on it—though he'd met no resistance from Angie. He'd wanted to demonstrate the depth and commitment of his feelings for her—and to sweep her off her feet.

In the small, grey-stone church near the Castellari castle, they had married on a beautiful spring day—with skies of brilliant blue and the swell of birdsong seeming to echo the swell of love in the bride's heart.

Soft tulle whispering over the worn flagstones, she had made her way to the altar, where her proud bride-groom awaited—with Todd marching behind her, in a little pageboy's outfit. Romano had been best man—darkly enigmatic and slightly disapproving, she fancied, but confident she would win him round. Deep down, Romano cared as much about families as Riccardo did—and he would ensure that his new sister-in-law was welcomed into theirs.

Only Floriana had not been in attendance—having been rushed to hospital with complications in the early stages of her honeymoon pregnancy. Angie had wanted to postpone the wedding, but Floriana and Max had refused to let her. And in the end, the alarm had proved false. Discharged into the care of her husband, Floriana had gone on to give birth to a beautiful, bouncing baby boy—and all the preceding arguments had been forgotten in the presence of this new life.

Riccardo had been smitten by his nephew, and so too had Romano. And Angie had been moved to tears when the couple had asked her to be their new baby's godmother.

Angie adjusted her hat one last time and turned t
look at her husband, heartbreakingly handsome in his
formal dark suit.

'You know what an honour this is, in an Italian
family?' he asked her tenderly as he came to stand
beside her at the window, putting his arm around her
shoulders. 'To be godmother to a firstborn?'

Angie picked up her handbag and nodded, her
luminous smile making her face appear radiant.

'Yes, I do,' she whispered. 'But I am honoured
anyway—to be part of this family, and more honoured
still to be your wife, my darling Riccardo.'

'No, the honour is mine,' he said simply, and as he
touched his lips to hers he sighed. 'Do you think it is
possible for us to be any happier, *cara mia*?'

She thought that it was very possible—and later she
would tell him why. When they had returned from
Rocco's baptism and were alone together in their suite
at the castle she would tell him the news she knew he
longed for.

But for now. One more kiss. Slow, leisurely, perfect.

Just like her life with Riccardo. Her love, her
soulmate, her equal.

Join Us!

The Community is the perfect place to meet and chat to kindred spirits who love books and reading as much as you do, but it's also the place to:

- **Get the inside scoop from authors about their latest books**
- **Learn how to write a romance book with advice from our editors**
- **Help us to continue publishing the best in women's fiction**
- **Share your thoughts on the books we publish**
- **Befriend other users**

Forums: Interact with each other as well as authors, editors and a whole host of other users worldwide.

Blogs: Every registered community member has their own blog to tell the world what they're up to and what's on their mind.

Book Challenge: We're aiming to read 5,000 books and have joined forces with The Reading Agency in our inaugural Book Challenge.

Profile Page: Showcase yourself and keep a record of your recent community activity.

Social Networking: We've added buttons at the end of every post to share via digg, Facebook, Google, Yahoo, technorati and de.licio.us.

www.millsandboon.co.uk

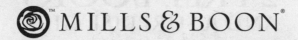

2 FREE BOOKS
AND A SURPRISE GIFT

We would like to take this opportunity to thank you for reading this Mills & Boon® book by offering you the chance to take TWO more specially selected books from the Modern™ series absolutely FREE! We're also making this offer to introduce you to the benefits of the Mills & Boon® Book Club™—

- **FREE home delivery**
- **FREE gifts and competitions**
- **FREE monthly Newsletter**
- **Exclusive Mills & Boon Book Club offers**
- **Books available before they're in the shops**

Accepting these FREE books and gift places you under no obligation to buy, you may cancel at any time, even after receiving your free books. Simply complete your details below and return the entire page to the address below. You don't even need a stamp!

YES Please send me 2 free Modern books and a surprise gift. I understand that unless you hear from me, I will receive 4 superb new books every month for just £3.19 each, postage and packing free. I am under no obligation to purchase any books and may cancel my subscription at any time. The free books and gift will be mine to keep in any case.

Ms/Mrs/Miss/Mr_____ Initials _____

Surname _____

Address _____

_____

_____ Postcode _____

Send this whole page to: Mills & Boon Book Club, Free Book Offer, FREEPOST NAT 10298, Richmond, TW9 1BR